&

Demigods

A Montague and Strong Detective Agency Novel

By

Orlando A. Sanchez

FOREWORD

In the course of writing a book, which for me, is usually a few months, life happens. Events unfold, some good, and some bad. I started writing dedications to honor those moments and people, to find some way to express my respect and heartfelt feelings for the pain and joy we all share, because we are all connected. We are all one.

Life and Death are inextricably intertwined. Sometimes as a writer, I think a book or story is about one thing when it's really about something else that blindsides you after the book is done. That happened to me with this book. I write primarily to entertain and to provide my amazing readers with a few moments of escape. I want to provide a few moments of light in what can be a very dark world.

Simon is an immortal and rather than having a casual or flippant attitude towards life, he is very aware that he can lose those closest to him, his family. That's not to say that he always approaches the subject seriously. Part of what makes him who he is, is that even in the face of danger and certain death, he can find a moment of lightness, much to Monty's aggravation.

That's what I want you to take away. When it seems like it's the end and there is no hope, find the light in the darkness. Even the faintest light can blaze like the sun in darkness. Be the light, we have enough darkness in this world.

Dedication

For every parent who has had to do the unthinkable

I wrote and deleted this dedication several times. Part of me felt it would make the book too dark. In the end, I felt I needed to say this because these parents need to be honored. Death is a part of life we can't avoid. I learned this fact very young.

I'm not going to mention any names because this wound never heals. Time doesn't make it easier and no words could ever convey the loss and constant pain of losing a child. I had to go into some very dark places to write the character of George Rott for this book. As a father, I felt his pain and understood his motivation. I know what it is to carry a casket for a child, and I wish it upon no one.

This dedication is to let all who have gone through this know that I understand your pain and loss. That you are not alone. Your daily battle with grief and anger has not gone unnoticed. There are no words that can aptly describe this experience and I won't try here.

On those days when it gets too heavy and life feels a little darker, remember: there are shoulders to rest on. We got you.

Dedication

For Chaos & Dizzy

My first dog, Juno, passed away when I was in my late teens. He woke up one day at the ripe old age of 16 and his hind legs decided they were done. No more walking. He looked at me, gave me a wag as if to say "I have to go, but it's going to be okay. You're going to be okay. We've had a massively great run, but it's time for me to leave."

He had been with me since he was eight weeks old and had been there for most of my life. I picked him up with tears in my eyes. We made a last trip to the vet. I held him as they put him to sleep and vowed to never feel that pain again. Fast forward twenty years and I have my awesome boxer, named Winter, and I'm looking at getting an actual Peaches to join the family.

I will always remember Juno fondly. He was a terrier-Tasmanian devil mutt that terrorized our neighborhood and I loved him fiercely. We still tell stories about him in our family. In that way he still lives on and is with us.

This dedication is for all those who have lost furry family members. They love us unconditionally, fill our days with laughter and sometimes groans, but we love them just the same and can't imagine our lives without them.

All fathers are invisible in daytime; daytime is ruled by mothers and fathers come out at night. Darkness brings home fathers, with their real, unspeakable power. There is more to fathers than meets the eye. -Margaret Atwood

So comes the snow after the fire and even dragons have their endings.-J.R.R. Tolkien

Published by Bitten Peaches Publishing NY NY

Cover Design by Deranged Doctor Design
www.derangeddoctordesign.com

ONE

"MONTY, ARE YOU certain this is necessary?" I looked up from the pile of reports on my desk.

He finished polishing his swords, the Sorrows, and resheathed them. A soft cry escaped the blades as they disappeared into the back cross-sheaths and vanished from sight.

"It's either this, or we risk angering the entire family. This is the best solution, Simon."

"You know we need to address this Rott situation before he does something that gets him killed and takes us along for the ride."

I remembered the last time I'd spoken to George Rott, Cassandra's father:

"You owe me, and you owe her."

"Listen, George, I don't know what you found, but why don't we meet to discuss this?"

"I found them," he whispered. *"I found the dragons."*

"We need to address this first." Monty pulled on

one of his sleeves, reached for a cup of tea sitting on the desk, and headed to the back room. "They should be here shortly."

"Is Dex coming?"

"He'll meet us there. We have guests to escort."

Between London and the Sanctuary, we hadn't been in the city for a week or so. Ramirez had been leaving me messages about strange activity downtown near the South Street Seaport. These events seemed to coincide with the increase in runic activity occurring near the Hellfire Club. I didn't like the timing, especially with George out hunting dragons.

If it had been just a grieving father, that would be one thing, but George 'Rottweiler' Rott had also led NYTF's Shadow Company—the company I served in a lifetime ago.

His skills made him dangerous and resourceful. He wasn't a man to be taken lightly in the best of circumstances. Now, he was blinded by revenge for his daughter. This was going to get ugly fast. I was about to pick up the phone to call Ramirez, when a knock interrupted me.

"That them?" I holstered Grim Whisper and sheathed Ebonsoul. Peaches rolled over, nearly crushing my legs. I tried shoving him over, but he didn't budge.

<You could lie down anywhere else in the office, you know.>

<I know. But your feet are warm.>

The knock sounded again.

"Unless you're expecting your vampire, I would imagine so," Monty called out. "I have one more item to secure before we leave. Can you let them in?"

I stood up and approached the door, when I saw the ice creep along the floor and enter the office.

"Monty? I think you need to get this one… unless we have a blowtorch handy?"

The temperature in the office dropped by about twenty degrees, and we entered a mini ice age as frost started to form on the door and creep around the frame.

"Are you ready?" he asked, walking up to the door.

"For what, frostbite?"

He glared at me, reminding me that our guests weren't exactly friendly. He gestured and formed an orb of flame around his hand as he opened the door.

Three of the most beautiful women I'd seen in my entire life stood at our door. Three sets of sky-blue eyes blazed at us with thinly-veiled violence behind them.

Each of their faces was framed by white-blond hair. The fact that I could see combat armor under their long white leather coats did little to put me at ease.

Their energy signatures were strong enough to give me pause. Ice mages made me nervous after our brief but homicidal encounter with the not-so-stable Steigh Cea.

I hoped her sisters weren't as prone to spontaneous violence. The center woman, who was the tallest of the three, stepped into our office. The remaining two turned their backs on us and stayed outside the door.

"Well met, Hekla," Monty said with a nod. "Are you ready?"

Hekla nodded and took in our office remaining silent for a few seconds. Her eyes lingered on Peaches and she sniffed with a hint of disgust. Maybe it was an ice-mage thing, but she had the condescending look down to an artform. I almost wanted to run to my room and straighten it up.

"I'm here to secure the runic neutralizer, mage," she said, her husky voice filling the office. "If I deem your location of choice to be inadequate, I will relocate it to our home, as per our agreement. My sisters will remain here until I return."

"Understood." Monty gestured and formed a large circle on the floor. "We will be traveling to Fordey Boutique. I have chosen them to keep the neutralizer safe, and I have some matters to attend to there."

"Proceed." She waved her hand as if we were boring her just by existing. "Do you need assistance with your circle?"

"Thank you for the offer, but I believe I can manage."

She looked down when Peaches stepped into the circle with us. "This infernal *thing* will be traveling with us?"

"He has a habit of following me around," I said, barely containing my anger. I rubbed Peaches' head, and he rumbled extra loudly. "It's better if *Peaches* joins us."

She stepped to the other side of the circle and nodded to Monty. "Carry on, mage."

Monty gestured as white runes floated around us. With a last sweep of his arm, the office disappeared.

TWO

WE STEPPED OUT of the circle and into what I assumed was Fordey Boutique. The last time I'd been here, all of the available floor space had been covered in boxes and crates. The walls had held warped shelves appearing to be on the verge of collapse. This time, all that was gone.

We stood in an open reception area the size of an enormous hotel lobby. A large, gleaming, golden X, outlined in red, dominated the center of the black marble floor. It reflected the light pouring in from a domed window set in the ceiling. I looked around, and wondered if we had taken a detour to a museum.

The only pieces furniture I saw were the white marble benches situated along the wall at even intervals. Small recessed alcoves were above each bench.

An intricately carved, white marble statue stood

inside each alcove. All of the statues were in action poses except for one. I walked over to that one and realized it was a statue of TK.

This statue stood with her hands resting on a sword, point down. Her legs were slightly apart and the lifelike expression on her face was a cross between a scowl and a smile, as if to say, 'step closer so I can shred you'.

I shuddered. The statue only captured a fraction of the intensity TK possessed. I moved around the room and examined some of the others. I found one for LD, Rene, and Jonno. I didn't recognize the rest of them, but I assumed this was a space dedicated to the Ten.

"This is Fordey?"

"Yes and no." Monty gestured and the circle beneath us vanished. "This is the Hall of the Ten. It's connected to Fordey through that corridor."

"What corridor?" I turned in the direction he pointed, and an archway materialized. "Oh, that corridor."

A figure stepped through the archway. She was dressed in a flowing white robe, which was covered in silver runic brocade. Her long, black hair cascaded behind her as she stood in the corridor without entering the Hall of the Ten.

"She's waiting for us to follow." Monty stepped forward and approached the woman.

"Is that a Wordweaver?"

"Yes." Monty, who was usually scowly, was going

for extra grim today. Even Hekla, who previously had appeared arrogant seemed humbled by the presence of the Wordweaver.

Peaches nudged my leg, nearly tearing my ACL, and rumbled.

<Do you have any meat?>

<No, I don't have any meat. Can you wait until we get home? You just ate.>

<That was a long time ago.>

<It was thirty minutes ago.>

<Like I said, a long time ago. You should carry meat with you. Your coat has pockets. I don't have pockets. Have you learned to make the magic meat yet?>

<No. Dex said he would teach me the spell. Right now, we have to do this.>

<Can I get meat after?>

<Yes. Monty said Dex would meet us here. I'll ask him to make some meat for you. Can you hold it together until then?>

<I'll try. Can I bite the tall lady if I get hungry?>

<No. No biting anyone unless I say so.>

He chuffed in response and padded off.

"What are Wordweavers doing in Fordey? Do you owe them a book?"

"No," he said with a sigh, "they are here to witness the Reckoning."

The Wordweaver turned and led the way once we entered the corridor.

"And the Reckoning needs witnesses because…?"

"In addition to the Triad, Wordweavers officiate, observe and, more importantly, enforce the rules established by the parties of a Reckoning. In this case, TK and myself."

TK's words came back to me: *Because of the regard in which I hold your uncle...blood and power.*

"Blood and power?"

"Yes, those are the conditions."

"That sounds painful. Can't you just do some community service here at the boutique? Stock some shelves or clean out the inventory? Maybe do a few delivery runs with LD?"

"No. This needs to happen. At least it's not to the death. That would put Uncle Dex in an awkward position. I'll need to remember to thank TK for that."

"That's your concern? Dex being put in an awkward position?"

"Yes. As a direct blood relative, he *must* stand by me during a Reckoning, but TK, LD, and the others are also his family, even if they're not blood. TK allowed him to fulfill his duty as my uncle without sacrificing his relationship with them. She allowed him to save face."

"As she rips off yours. TK is powerful, Monty." I looked ahead at the Wordweaver. "Does she know where she's going? I don't remember the boutique being this large."

"Time and relative dimension in space aren't fixed constructs in Fordey Boutique. This design is based on the Corridors of Chaos. I doubt she'll get lost here."

The Wordweaver led us down several corridors in silence. Hekla must have sensed we were in a magical construct. She kept her distance but didn't let us get too far away from her. It was either that or she didn't like being near Peaches, who rumbled at her every time she got too close.

"Can you forfeit?"

"No. This isn't a game. To forfeit would be an affront to TK and a loss of face for my uncle. He'd kill me if I forfeited. He's quite touchy about the family name."

"Yes, he's a bit of a traditionalist, even though the family doesn't really like him. How many Montagues are there?"

"Our family is not very large, but we are influential in the mage community. With the death of my father, Uncle Dex will have to assume some responsibility at the Sanctuary."

"I bet he's going to love that."

"It can't be helped. A Montague has been an Elder in the Sanctuary since its inception." He brushed some hair out of his face. "In any case, I tried to tether a Smith Bridge to TK and must face the consequences of my actions."

"You did what you thought was best, considering the circumstances. It was a horrible idea, but I get it. The no-forfeit clause sucks, though."

"There's another reason I can't forfeit," he added. "A forfeit could shift the conditions from blood and power to death."

"But TK wouldn't take it that far, right? Would she?"

"It would be out of her hands at that point. The Triads hold the right to determine the new condition in the event of a forfeit."

"Who makes up these Triads?" I looked around. "Is it Dex, Peaches, and me?"

"A mage, an immortal, and a shifter have to form the Triad. You can't be part of the Triad."

"But I'm an—?"

"As my shieldbearer," he said with a look that meant 'shut up before you divulge something important,' "you can't be part of the Triad. I've found a substitute."

"What about TK? Does she need this 'Triad' group too?"

He nodded. "Yes, that's the tradition, to ensure the rules of the Reckoning are observed."

"Six powerful individuals in a room watching a fight. That doesn't sound like a recipe for disaster at all."

The Wordweaver made a few more turns and led us down several dimly lit corridors. Most of them had shelving of some kind holding all sorts of items. At the end of one of these corridors, we came to another thick steel door.

"We're here." Monty reached back and drew the

Sorrows, handing them to the Wordweaver. "Keep your eyes open and your creature in check."

"No weapons?"

"This is a Reckoning of mages. No conventional weapons are permitted."

"This door looks familiar…this is the—"

"Danger Room," said a voice from behind us. "Welcome back, gentlemen and guest."

It was LD. He held a black cat in his arms as he approached. The cat's coat shone with latent energy and its eyes glowed with a subtle yellow light.

"LD, it's good to see you." I looked down. The cat's eyes glowed brighter. "I don't remember you having a…I want to say cat?"

"Hello, Tristan, Simon," he replied, stroking the cat on his arm, his voice serious, matching his expression. I noticed he was dressed in a black suit, and I got a distinct Bond-villain vibe. "This is Dinger, short for Chaos T. Schrodinger."

"Dinger? Really?" The cat-creature was giving me the 'clearly I'm superior to you' look with glowing eyes so I kept my distance.

"If you look around here, you'll see his partner in crime, Diz, short for Discord. Just don't try and pet her."

"Another feline?"

"No, that one looks like a beagle, but don't be fooled. She's really a singularity disguised as a dog. If you see her, walk away. And whatever you do, don't feed her."

"What? She transforms? Should I avoid getting her wet, too?"

"Simon, does it look like I'm joking? Do not feed her. She'll make your hellhound look like he's on a hunger strike. The last time someone did, we lost part of the boutique."

"Fine, I won't feed your black-hole beagle. What's this look?" I pointed at the cat. "Blofeld lite?"

"Hilarious as a heart attack, *hombre*." LD placed the cat on the floor. It purred by his feet, staring at me.

"When did you get a—is it a cat? The glowing eyes make me want to say no."

"He's an interstitial feline. Pretty rare."

"An intestinal what?

"*Interstitial*, not intestinal."

"An *interstitial* feline? It's between—?"

"Planes." The cat disappeared a second later and he brushed off his suit. "They travel between planes. Sort of like what your hellhound does in short bursts, except Dinger is what's known as a Planewalker."

I looked around but didn't see the cat anywhere. "Where'd he go?"

"Don't know." LD shrugged. "Wherever he wants. He's never really gone for long. He's TK's, so he usually stays with her when he's here, but because of the Reckoning, I get to watch him."

Monty gave LD a short nod. "My Triad?"

"Inside and ready." LD gestured and gray runes formed in the air. "We're waiting for the last member of TK's to arrive. In the meantime, I'll take your guest to the neutralizer. Hekla is it?"

Monty nodded and stepped to the side, allowing Hekla to join LD.

"She would like to ascertain the security of the neutralizer. If she's not satisfied, I told her she's free to take it back to her home."

"I understand." LD gestured again and opened a rift. "She's welcome to test the security as much as she can bear. I'm sure she'll find it satisfactory."

Hekla raised an eyebrow and sniffed. "I will determine the state of the neutralizer, not you." She stepped into the rift, disappearing. LD looked back and gave me a nod.

"This is going to be a short test. Be right back." He followed her in and the rift closed behind him.

"Do we wait here?" I turned to Monty, who had his eyes closed.

"Yes. LD is TK's shieldbearer. He will escort us in, and then after the formalities, we'll begin."

Ten minutes later, I felt a shift in the energy around us. Another rift opened, and a smiling LD stepped through, followed by a disheveled Hekla. Her hair was all over the place. It looked like she had been standing in a wind tunnel for the last ten minutes. Her expression of arrogance and superiority had been transformed to one of shock and surprise. I almost felt sorry for her.

She gave Monty a tight nod and a bow.

"Is the security adequate?" Monty looked at her with a raised eyebrow, channeling his inner Vulcan. "Does it meet with your approval?"

"Yes," she managed, after taking a few seconds to compose herself and smooth out her hair. "The security is adequate. We will leave the neutralizer under your responsibility in Fordey Boutique."

"Thank you for entrusting me with such a delicate artifact," Monty said, returning the bow. "I will make sure it is kept safe."

"It…it is very safe." She gestured with a shaking hand, forming a teleportation circle, which collapsed a few seconds later.

It reminded me of my adventures with the Incantation of Light. My magic-missile orbs suffered from the same condition, premature energy expulsion. In my case, it was a matter of inexperience. For Hekla, an ice mage, the loss of concentration required for her to miss a basic teleportation spell meant she was mentally out of it.

Monty stepped closer to her. "Do you need assistance with your circle?"

She tried to gesture again, failed, and gave him one distinct, slight nod. I can only imagine the difficulty and humility it took for her to execute that nod.

Monty returned her nod and bowed. "Thank

you for allowing me the honor of assisting you in this task." He gestured and formed a teleportation circle. "This will return you to my home and remain long enough to transport you and your sisters to your home."

"You have my gratitude, Tristan Montague." She stepped into the circle. "I can see now why my sister held you in such high regard. I am ready."

Tristan nodded again and gestured, and Hekla, elder sister of the Jotnar, disappeared.

"What happened to her?" I looked at LD, who was smiling and shaking his head. "What did you do?"

"Me? I didn't do anything." LD held his hands up in surrender. "She tried to remove the neutralizer from the artifact room."

Monty shook his head. "How far did she get?"

"We used the neutralizer to reset the Black Heart. It took both TK *and* I to calibrate it correctly. I even had to consult Ziller to make sure we didn't shift this plane out of existence. It now keeps the room and Fordey in a paradoxed juxtaposition across every plane."

"Did it give her a headache? Wait, how did you consult Ziller? I thought he was in the Repository back at the Sanctuary?"

"He is, but he's keeping it untethered. Said it was safer this way. He mentioned something about keeping it at the Sanctuary for certain hours and then moving it."

"Like the Moving Market?"

"On steroids," LD added. "He can make the Repository appear anywhere or anywhen. This is Professor Ziller we're talking about."

"So the Black Heart stopped her?"

"You could say that," LD said with a chuckle. "She took a few steps in and suddenly found herself face to face with all of the Heklas across a thousand parallel universes."

"How did that stop her? She's an ice mage."

"The moment she stepped into the temporal wave of the Black Heart, she was scattered across the planes. Doesn't matter what kind of magic you wield, that experience can shatter your mind. If I hadn't pulled her out, she'd be lost *and* insane."

"No wonder she looked like a wreck. I wonder what she saw."

"She experienced hundreds of lifetimes in the span of a few seconds. That sort of thing can undo a mind. I don't think she'll be back to 'test' the security of the neutralizer again."

The vault door opened, and another Wordweaver stepped into the corridor. "The Triads are now complete. We may commence."

LD put a hand on Monty's shoulder. "TK is going to make this hurt like hell." He looked away for a second. "Understand the source and realize it'll be over...eventually. Even if it doesn't feel like it."

Monty nodded. "I understand the source."

LD looked at me and then down at Peaches. "Let's go. Shieldbearers go in first."

"First? What do you mean we go in first? What are we supposed to do?"

"Just follow my lead."

THREE

THE VAULT DOOR was covered in black runes and gave off a 'run away now while you can' vibe. LD gestured and the runes covering the door disappeared as we crossed the threshold. We stepped inside, and I noticed not much had changed since my last visit.

The far wall still held a few craters in an odd sequence, and the ceiling was covered in jagged valleys. On the wall closest to me, I saw what appeared to be blast residue. Peaches' eye-beam trench was a fresh addition to the destruction.

Opposite the door, on the far side of the floor, sat seven chairs on a dais obscured in shadow. I had a brief flashback to the Penumbra Consortium and shuddered. Ever since London, daises and mages made me uncomfortable.

Wordweavers stood in every corner. Their white robes had brocades of red and gold, which meant they were Master Weavers. Their impassive faces betrayed no emotion and kicked up the creepy vibe a few notches.

"Don't you ever fix this room?" I looked around at the wholesale destruction. "Place still looks like a warzone."

"It's a Danger Room. It's meant to look like this, because I actually use it for dangerous items. It's not a glorified meeting place."

"Like the Hall of the Ten?"

"Don't even get me started on that…not my idea." He grumbled. "Who needs a room full of statues of themselves? Ego much?"

I looked around. "Well, this place could use a renovation. At least fix the destruction so no one trips."

"We will in a sec," LD said. "It was a logistical nightmare, arranging to have Fordey as the site of the Reckoning. TK refused to go overseas."

"Why? It would have been easy to port over or create a rift. Even a flight…"

"Her choice, and she won't fly. Something about her last flight being enough of an adventure to last her a few centuries." He glanced knowingly at me. "Since she called for the Reckoning, she had the choice of location. We were just waiting for everyone to get here before casting."

Figures assembled on the dais and began sitting in the large chairs. The light made it hard to make out who was sitting where.

"Is this the way it's settled between mages?"

"No, back in the day, when two mages fought, they would find a deserted field and battle until only one walked away. Which was fine, except it wasn't always a deserted field, and not every mage fought honorably. The Reckonings were created to stop the power plays."

"And the destruction to populated areas, I'm sure."

"Better to contain the destruction than have to deal with authorities and cleanup. Not that you or Tristan would ever unleash unimaginable amounts of power inside a populated city or anything."

"Why does everyone assume I have something to do with the destructive forces of a mage?"

"Good question. Maybe we should ask René while she waits for her new Strix?"

"That was Dex's fault."

"Funny, I don't remember Dex forming the orb that punched through the plane. How does that saying go?" A smile briefly crossed his lips. "When it happens once, it's an accident, when it happens as often as it does to you and Tristan, I call that a way of life. But hey, whatever lets you sleep at night."

I remained silent and took in the proceedings. Most of the figures were seated, and some of the Wordweavers moved around the dais and the floor.

The room was about half the size of a typical high-school gymnasium. The wooden floors were surprisingly intact, given the state of the rest of the room. Bright sunlight cascaded in from the large, thick, barred windows high up on one of the walls. The smell of old wood and lemon wax filled my lungs, transporting me back to my teens for a moment.

Power emanated from the room. I wondered if the addition of the neutralizer enhanced or augmented the power I felt. It had a subtle undertone of barely contained destruction. Even with all of that, the power felt in the Danger Room paled in comparison to the brain-crushing force of the artifact in the Black Heart room.

This power was subtle and enveloped me. I turned, trying to find the source, but couldn't pinpoint it. I noticed the pulsing of the subtle runes covering the walls and floors. The entire room was giving off waves of ambient energy.

The last time I was here, it was a large open space with only one entrance. This time I noticed there were two additional entrances on either side of the room. I wondered how large Fordey Boutique really was.

Once all the figures were seated, LD stepped to the center of the floor and motioned for me to join him. I stepped next to him, and he cleared his throat.

He faced the seven people and bowed, elbowing me in the side to remind me I was supposed to bow with him.

"The Triads are complete," he said once we finished bowing. "We can commence the Reckoning."

The woman in the center stood and stepped forward, apart from the other six. She wore a golden robe with red brocade. Runes glimmered on the fabric of the robe. She must have been one of the leaders of the Wordweavers to wear that robe. She returned LD's bow and began gesturing. She looked vaguely familiar, but I couldn't place her face or the voice.

"Shieldbearers, please take your designated places while I prepare the combat area."

LD and I walked over to the designated area beside the dais. Two Wordweavers bookended us as we stood next to the wall. I looked up and was able to make out the faces of the seated figures.

I saw what I guessed to be Monty's Triad. Dex sat between Michiko and Jimmy the Butcher. All of them wore formal attire, looked deadly serious, and ignored my attempt to get their attention.

I was about to wave at them when the woman in the golden robe gave me a 'get it together' look, and the realization hit.

"Oh, shit," I said under my breath, lowering my arm slowly. "That's Dahvina?"

LD nodded. "This is a big deal. She *requested* to officiate this Reckoning. Usually it's just one of the Master Weavers." He glanced at a corner. "I saw at least ten of them, not counting Dahvina."

"She's the leader of the Wordweavers. Why would she be here?"

"The Montagues are well known and respected in the mage community. Except for Dex, he's kind of infamous."

"That much I can believe."

"And TK is, well…TK. She's one of the Ten. The Wordweavers wouldn't exist without the Ten. We saved their asses."

"You what?" I said, keeping my voice low. "How did you do that?"

"Long story for a different time."

"Who's that?" I pointed with my chin over to the tall man in TK's Triad. "I don't recognize him."

"You wouldn't. That's Kristman Dos. He's a weretiger. Leader of Eastern Streak and one of the Ten. He's ferocious and deadly, keeps mostly to himself unless we have a mission."

"The Eastern Streak sounds like a basketball team."

LD stared at me for a good five seconds before speaking. "When you go out on these adventures with Tristan and Dex, do you get hit in the head a lot?"

"No more than usual, why?"

"Sometimes you sound brain-damaged," LD said with a shake of his head and a sigh.

"Monty says the same thing, just without words."

"I bet. Anyway a streak is a group of tigers. The

Eastern Streak is a pack of weretigers that stretches along the Eastern Seaboard of the United States from Maine to Florida. He leads them."

"That must be a lot of weretigers."

"Last time we checked, it was eight hundred strong, probably close to over a thousand by now."

"He basically leads an army of weretigers?"

LD nodded. "An army that has declared him fit to lead. Weretigers are not democratic."

I looked over to where Chi sat. Her face was a stone mask. "Neither are vampires. Only the strongest, most cunning, and ruthless can lead."

"Well, he's the one we were waiting for. I don't know how they found him. He's been missing for over a year- running with the streak, doing who knows what."

Kristman Dos wore an Armani slate gray suit, no tie, finished off with a pair of Hermes Rafael loafers. His salt-and-pepper hair hung to his shoulders, and his eyes gleamed orange when he looked in my direction. His expression was one of amused boredom, but his eyes held an intense ferocity. It made sense that he was part of TK's Triad.

"A mage, a shifter, and an immortal. He's the shifter, who are the other two?"

The energy in the room fluctuated, and I saw trails of white runes flow from Dahvina's hands.

"You'd better watch yourself and hold on to something. Wordweavers can get carried away when casting."

"What's she doing?"

"Preparing the room for combat. I told her I would do it, but she insisted, and TK agreed." He shook his head and held on to the railing near the dais. "This is going to be over the top, just wait."

The destruction in the walls and ceiling repaired itself. The floor transformed from wood to gleaming white marble. The walls transformed to pink marble to coordinate with the floor. The dais rose several feet as a marble platform materialized under it and the entire floor sank about a foot. It gave the room a gladiatorial feel, if gladiators fought in the halls of a museum.

"That's quite a change." I looked around at the newly redone Danger Room. The polished marble shone in the sunlight. Runes danced across the floors and walls in strange and erratic patterns. "Can they come in here and make changes like they own the place?"

"We refused to be owned," LD said with a grin. "But I can be rented if the price is right."

"You're worse than Dex."

Braziers burning incense stood next to the dais, filling the room with the heady smell of lotus blossoms. For a second, I panicked, checking my mark to make sure I hadn't accidentally pressed it and summoned Karma.

"Now I won't get that smell out of here for a week," LD grumbled. "She does this every time."

"She totally went upscale Roman Coliseum on the remodel. What's that smell?"

"Dahvina's favorite scent, Karmic Lotus."

"At least the marble is a nice touch." I looked around at the Danger Room.

"Right, because marble is a great fighting surface. You ever fall on marble? Get thrown on marble?"

I winced. "A few times, yes."

"How'd that feel? Was it good times? Did you enjoy the bounce?"

"Not so much. Right up there with the wonderful sensation of road rash from sliding on concrete bare-chested."

"Exactly. Wordweavers, powerful as they are, tend to choose form over function. Excuse me a moment."

LD walked over to the dais and motioned to Dahvina, who approached warily. Clearly, he wasn't in awe of her position or power. I wondered who the Ten really were to command such respect, even from the Wordweavers.

I looked around the newly transformed Danger Room, but I didn't see TK. I knew Monty had been taken into an adjoining room until the formalities were over. They must have done the same with her.

LD strolled over with a smile on his face.

"Did she listen to your suggestion?"

"I reminded her that this was a Danger Room,

not her lobby in London, and that we're about to start a Reckoning, not a fashion show. In addition, as upscale as it looks, a marble floor is damn slippery for actual combat."

"So it's going to be wood again?"

"We came to a compromise."

I saw Dahvina gesture again. Another shift in energy filled the room. The center of the floor transformed from marble to a large rectangle of fine pink sand, bordered and separated from the main floor by rune-covered black marble. Two raised, semi-circular areas formed the center of the longest legs of the rectangle. She gave LD a short nod, which he returned.

"Is that going to be large enough?" I looked at what I assumed was the fighting area. It was about twice the size of a tennis court. "Pink sand? Really?"

LD shrugged. "That's plenty of room. I told her she could make it any color she wanted. She said something about aesthetics. I stopped paying attention after she agreed."

I looked back at the dais. "Who are the other two?"

"You don't recognize the woman?" LD asked with a smile. "You should. That's Badb Catha, the Boiling One."

The woman wore a black flowing gown and a headdress that partially covered her face. Red energy flowed around her body in tight circles.

"Bob who?"

"Look closer, but not too close. I don't feel like cleaning up a mess."

"A mess?" I turned to face the woman. "What the hell are you talking about?"

I let my senses expand and focused on her. Immediately, a sense of dread clutched my chest, making it hard to breathe. The dread was stomped on and kicked to the side by the overwhelming fear that took its place.

"Easy, *hombre*." LD grabbed my arm, steadying me. "I said not too close."

I was still looking at her when she turned her head slightly in my direction and gave me a Mona Lisa smile. Her smile was the promise of death and glory, victory and sacrifice, agony and mind-numbing pain. It made me want to claw my eyes out and run, screaming, out of the room.

LD yanked me back and turned me away from her. I heard Peaches whine and rumble by my side.

"That's the…the Morrigan," I said, my voice trembling.

"One aspect of the three, the super scary one." He gestured, and I saw gray runes cascade on my face and head. "I told you not to look too closely, and you think it's a staring contest? That's a good way to get your brain fried."

"That's not the Morrigan I usually see with Dex," I said after catching my breath. "That one is just moderately nightmarish. This one is in full-blown apocalypse mode."

"She's the *immortal* of TK's Triad. They go back a few centuries. A very dark, scary part of TK's past I'd rather not get into."

"TK knows her?"

LD nodded. "They sort of worked together for a while. I can't really go into detail, and, trust me, you don't want to know. TK's the reason Dex is with the Morrigan. Well, not this aspect of her, but you know what I mean."

"What the hell was Monty thinking, trying to tether a Smith Bridge to TK?"

"He wasn't thinking. I know he was concerned, his father being involved and all, but he's lucky Dex is his uncle. If anyone else had tried that with TK, we would be burying the remains. TK doesn't like it when *I* ask her where she's going...*inside* the boutique. He was trying to tether a Smith Bridge to her. There's a word for that where I come from."

"Reckless? Idiotic?"

"Suicidal."

"How can the Morrigan look like this and the other way the way she is with Dex? You know, nightmare lite?"

"The Morrigan is a triune goddess. She's made up of three aspects: Morrigan, Badb, and Macha. Sometimes the names change, but she's always had three aspects."

"Why is she here like that?" My hands were still shaking. "This isn't a battlefield."

"This is a Reckoning, and that aspect is the one she uses for battles. That's why it's called Badb Catha, the battle crow. She strikes fear and confusion in her enemies. Think of this as her dressing up for the affair."

"Her formal wear is a fear-inducing monster version of herself?" I kept my voice low while crouching down next to Peaches.

"Something like that. Just keep your distance, and don't try to gauge her energy signature. Even Dex gives her space when she's like this, and they have a 'thing' going on."

"He must really be insane." I rubbed Peaches' head. His rumble-whine was still going.

<It's okay, boy. The scary lady is just here to make sure the rules are followed. Don't worry. I'm good.>

<I'm not worried. It's just been a long time since I've had meat.>

I looked at his face and shook my head.

<Good to know you're concerned about me. I nearly lost it a minute ago.>

<Lost what? Meat? You have meat?>

<Nevermind.>

"Dex was never right in the head, but he's family to us," LD said after a moment. "I'm glad TK picked blood and power." He raised a hand quickly. "I mean, I'm not looking forward to Tristan's pounding, but if it has to happen, blood and power is better than death."

"Blood and power." I glanced up at the dais. "I

know those are the conditions, but what does it mean?"

"No weapons, conventional or otherwise. Blood can be spilled, but no lethal wounds. They can use only their inherent power, no assists from anything or anyone."

"Monty's in trouble, isn't he? A creative mage can make and unmake any attack he comes up with."

"Let's just say TK is a lot older than Tristan. She has actual combat experience, like he does. She's fought very scary people, creatures, and...things. She's come out on the other side, harder and more dangerous."

"So, Monty's in trouble."

LD nodded. "Out of the Ten, she took the hardest, most insane missions. Facing off against a horde of angry demons looking to tear you to pieces? Call TK. Have an ogre or troll problem? Even better, have an ogre *and* troll situation? Call TK. We started calling her the Kamikaze."

"Which definition? Divine wind or suicidal bomber?"

"Elements of both. If she felt slighted or the target had acted unjustly, she was a divine wind of retribution. Other times, she would just rush into certain death without thinking. She's mellowed a bit with time."

"She's mellowed now?" I thought back to how she handled the Ghosts in this same room. If that was mellowed, I'd hate to see her being harsh.

LD nodded. "I'm just glad this Reckoning isn't to the death."

"I agree, because I'm pretty sure Monty would be on the losing end of that fight." I felt better and managed to glance at the dais. The third figure had to be the mage.

LD shook his head. "I don't know. Montagues are powerful mages. Tristan hasn't even tapped a fourth of his potential, and he's still young." He looked at the dais. "Dex could easily have joined the Ten if he wanted to."

"Who's the third figure?" I looked at the mage with the pupil-less eyes. "Is he another one of the Ten?"

LD's face darkened, as he grabbed my arm and squeezed. "Listen to me, Simon. If you think Badb Catha is scary, he makes her look like a Girl Scout —she's a homicidal, battle-crazy, blood-lusting, fear-inducing, psychotic battlefield goddess of war. I would still prefer to deal with her than him."

I heard real fear in LD's voice. He shook my arm as I started to glance at the dais. I stared at him, and he stared back, hard.

"He's bad news. I got it." I tried to pry my arm away from his vise-like grip and failed. "Can I have my arm back?"

"No, he's not 'bad news,' he's the worst news. He's one of the Soul Renderers and, no, he's not one of the Ten."

"Soul Renderer? That sounds friendly. I'm guessing dark mage?"

"Exactly. His name is Mahnes, and you stay away from him, no matter what. Do you understand?"

"Why is he here? I mean, I know *why* he's here, but how is he connected to TK? How is he the mage of her Triad?"

"A long time ago when Mahnes was more human than…whatever he is now, he and TK fought. She beat him and spared his life, even though she didn't have to."

"So he owes her." I glanced over at the dais again.

"A life debt." LD nodded and looked over at the dais too. "He went on to mess with dark magic that transformed him. He's a powerful mage and remembers that she spared him. You ask me, she should have dusted him when she had the chance."

"Why didn't she? He sounds like a real threat."

"It's complicated. TK is complicated. She felt it would be unfair. Now he's a Soul Renderer. They are almost impossible to kill."

"Does that make him immortal?"

"It makes him lethal." He finally let go of my arm, and the circulation returned to my fingers. "Stay away from him."

Dahvina finished redecorating the Danger Room. She whispered something and clapped her hands together. The sound of the clap reverberated throughout the room, making the floor vibrate around us.

"Commence the Reckoning." Dahvina's voice had the same effect as the clap, bouncing off the walls in mini echoes.

Two Master Weavers entered the Danger Room from archways on opposite sides of the room.

"I don't remember there being other entrances into the Danger Room the last time I was here."

"There weren't, and for good reason. I designed the room with one entrance and one exit to contain any dangerous artifact or ancient magic I might unleash."

"That makes sense. The archways look pretty, though."

"They're pointless and add nothing to a 'Danger Room' except liability." He shook his head. "Typical Wordweaver. The runes are useless now. They operated with the integrity of a contained space. Not"—he waved his hand around—"all of this."

"You can change it back, right? After the Reckoning?"

"Yes, but the balance of the room is off now. Any spells they cast will be affected."

"Affected how?"

"That would take me several hours to explain. Just be alert, and duck when needed."

"You'd think Dahvina would take that into account when she made the changes, right?"

He stared at me with a look that said 'can you

really be that dense?"

"Have you been paying attention to anything I've said about Wordweavers? Form over function? Just keep your eyes open. As a shieldbearer, you have to—"

"Have to what? I'm not a mage, and you've seen my 'magic.'"

"Yes, we still discuss your *magic missile*," he said with a tight smile. "Anyway, as shieldbearer, you have to maintain the integrity of the combat area."

"What exactly does that mean, 'maintain the integrity' of the combat area?"

"It means no one else can be in the combat area while TK and Tristan are fighting. No one except us two, and we won't really be inside of it. Not even your hellhound can step on the sand. Make sure he stays out."

I looked down at Peaches.

<You heard him?>

<Yes, I can't step on the sand in the area of fighting. What if someone drops a piece of meat? Can I enter then?>

<No one is going to be dropping meat, you black hole.>

<But if someone does? Can I get it?>

<If someone drops a piece of meat in the middle of the fight, feel free to get it and eat it. Until that happens, you don't go in unless I say so.>

He chuffed and sat on his haunches, looking alert.

"He won't go in. What happens if someone else

gets in the combat area?" I asked, not wanting to hear the answer. "Do they call a time out?"

"This isn't a basketball game, Simon. If anyone or anything violates the combat area, the Triads are free to act." He looked over at the dais. "Imagine those six going head to head on the floor."

"There wouldn't be much floor, boutique, or anything left." I glanced quickly at the dais. "Can't you or Dahvina put a barrier or something around the combat area?"

"Yes, that's us. We're the shieldbearers. Now, stay alert. Here they come."

FOUR

TWO MORE WORDWEAVERS appeared in the new archways on the sides of the room. They stepped into the Danger Room and moved to the side. Behind them stood Monty and TK in their respective archways.

Dahvina motioned, and they both entered the Danger Room in silence. She pointed at us, and LD nudged me. We walked to the center of the floor and stood in front of Monty and TK.

TK had her black hair pulled back in a tight ponytail, and I noticed small arcs of black energy jumping off her body. Monty was wearing a black pressed Zegna suit with a crisp white shirt and no tie. This was what I liked to call his mage uniform. White and violet runes floated around him in lazy orbits. The energy coursing through the room between the two of them set my teeth on edge.

I noticed TK's black combat armor was covered

in violet runes that crackled with power with every step she took. I was about to point out how this may be unfair when I saw Monty's suit do the same thing.

LD looked at me. "No unfair advantages," he said under his breath. "Both garments are laced with dragonscale and are runically enhanced."

We faced the dais. Dahvina had returned to her center seat and, with a hand, beckoned for us to step closer.

"Who bears their shields?"

I looked around, and LD stepped forward, extending a hand to indicate me. "We do." He reached into his shirt and pulled out an exact replica to the enso pendant I wore. His gave off a faint gray light. I reached under my shirt and pulled out the one given to me by Nana. It gave off a faint violet light. It felt heavier somehow. I looked up and saw Dahvina nod and gesture. A white rune floated over from her hand. It landed on the floor, causing all of the runes in the Danger Room to flare.

"The conditions of this Reckoning are blood and power. If those conditions are violated, the Reckoning will be declared void, and the offending mage or mages responsible will face the consequences, as determined by this body. Do any object?"

The silence expanded to fill the room.

"Very well, if no one—" Dahvina started.

"A word." It was Badb. Her voice carried surprisingly well across the danger-room floor. She sounded just like the Morrigan, which I should have expected. What I didn't expect was the cold grip of fear that followed her words. "May I?"

Dahvina gave Badb a short nod and pointed, allowing her to stand in the center of the dais. The temperature of the room dropped enough for me to see my breath on every exhalation.

"This battle pleases me." Badb nodded at Monty and TK. "If this Reckoning is violated in any way by any entity" —she paused to look at those seated on the dais—"they will experience the full force of my displeasure."

I don't know what was scarier. The goddess of battle endorsing the Reckoning, or her subtly threatening everyone on the dais. Badb returned to her seat with a nod to Dahvina. The leader of the Wordweavers walked over to Badb and spoke in a low whisper.

"I've always been told to judge someone by their friends," I said under my breath. "TK has some insanely scary friends."

"I know, right?" LD said with a grin. "Who are you bondmates with again? Oh right, a hellhound that manages to grow to the size of a small bus and that fires beams from his eyes, and a mage who unleashes world-ending spells in a city—not scary at all."

"That's different. The scary came with the

package."

"What? You think those six"—he nodded to the dais—"had to learn how to be scary?"

I felt the room temperature return to normal. Dahvina sat in her chair and looked at us. "Shieldbearers, to the combat area."

"I'm going to be standing on the opposite side." LD pointed across the floor. "Do exactly as I do. The pendants are primed to serve their functions. All you have to do is focus on the shield."

I nodded without understanding what he meant. I saw LD cross the combat area and step up onto the raised section. He placed a hand on his pendant and spread his arms wide. I did the same.

I placed a hand on my pendant and energy rushed through my body, forcing my arms to the side, keeping them rigid. I imagined this was what electrocution felt like, only with magic. I couldn't lower my arms or move my body. I felt the energy expand and travel down my arms. The runes in the black marble pulsed with violet light.

I saw the same thing happening across from me with LD. His face tensed as the energy flowed from his body, traveling along the edges of the combat area and meeting in the center, forming a barrier.

"Begin," Dahvina said. Her voice did that echoey thing again, and I focused on the pair in the center of the combat area.

I'd never really given much thought to what kind

of mage Monty was. I knew there were several types of magic-users, and that they each had their disciplines of study and practice. I recalled some of the magic-users we had faced. Some had off-the-charts power, like Hades. Even though, as a god, I don't think he qualified as a magic-user.

Others were very narrow in their discipline and expression of magic use, like Beck the Negomancer. He was a user of anti-magic. I remembered Monty saying TK and LD were creative mages. A very rare discipline of magic. Similar to Wordweavers, except where Wordweavers use the spoken word, creative mages used gestures to create—or undo.

I had only seen Monty manipulate elements and, of course, the void vortex, which almost got us killed on more than one occasion. Other than that, it was one of the four elements. On the other hand, TK was a creative mage, and I had seen her undo Ghosts. Creative magic sounded broad and dangerous.

TK stepped to the far side of the pink sand and looked at Monty, who had taken the opposite position. TK was much older than Monty, but Monty had recently absorbed part of his father's magical essence. Connor Montague had been an Elder of the Sanctuary and had been close to being an Arch Mage.

I didn't know if that directly translated to Monty being stronger, especially against TK. I had a feeling she was stronger than any of us imagined.

"Before we begin,"—Monty pulled on a sleeve, adjusting it—"I'd like to apologize for my actions and thank you for the selection of the conditions."

"You're welcome. Even though the conditions are blood and power, I suggest you don't restrain yourself, Tristan."

"I had no intention of doing so."

"Good."

A smile crossed her face, and she disappeared.

FIVE

MONTY GESTURED AND formed a shield. Several black orbs crashed into it, pushing him back. TK reappeared behind him and unleashed a black wave of energy. Monty created a blast of air, pointed it at the ground, and slid to the side to avoid the wave.

With a flick of her wrist, TK created several dozen orbs around her body. They crackled with black energy as they floated near her. Monty narrowed his eyes, placing his palms together. TK gestured again, and the orbs raced at Monty.

He stood there motionless, and I wondered if he intended on becoming an orb punching-bag. There was no way he could avoid all those orbs. I winced as they slammed into him, sending his body rolling across the sand.

TK walked over to Monty's body but kept her distance. I heard him groan.

"Those percussive orbs are quite formidable," he said with a gasp.

TK cocked her head to the side. "I expected more from you, Tristan. Your uncle will be disappointed."

"More from me, or more of me?"

"Excuse me?"

She rotated her body, avoiding a violet orb that shot past her. Another orb slammed into her side and knocked her on her back. I looked around and started seeing several Montys appear in the combat area.

TK stood with a smile. "You created casting simulacra. I'm impressed." She looked around the floor. "This is quite advanced."

"Thank you," I heard the voices of several Montys respond at once. "I've been practicing."

A few of the Montys bowed. One blew a raspberry at her. Some of them took defensive stances. There were so many, I couldn't tell which was the real one. They were all identical. When I tried to read the energy signatures, they all felt like the original, which was impossible.

TK swept an arm in front of her, and half the Montys disappeared. She raised an eyebrow and looked down. The runes on the floor had started pulsing.

"You're phasing them." She narrowed her eyes, gesturing. "Clever."

I saw more Montys replace the ones who had

been by TK's swipe. The Montys surrounded her, gesturing rapidly. She swiped an arm down as twenty violet beams focused on her. None of the beams reached her as she turned slowly, looking among the mass of Montys. I noticed one of the Montys starting to cough.

She pointed at the coughing Monty, and a black beam of energy shot from her finger, hitting him square in the chest. He flew back, slamming into the barrier.

The other Montys turned and ran to provide cover for the fallen Monty. Several of them gave TK angry glares as they stood in front of him. He got to his feet slowly, dusting sand off his sleeves. That was the real Monty.

"Once we began, I placed a minor irritant in the air. Slow acting and keyed to your signature."

"Clever," Monty answered between coughs. He gestured, placing his hand on his chest and suffusing himself with golden light. He took a deep breath and exhaled. "Much better."

TK knelt, placed both hands on the floor, and spoke. Monty raised an eyebrow, gestured, and crossed his arms in front of his body. White runes surrounded and enveloped him.

A black wave raced across the floor. I remembered this spell. It was a negation wave. TK had used it on the Ghosts the last time I was here getting Peaches a collar.

"Look out!" I yelled, but no sound escaped my

lips. Whatever energy I was channeling into the barrier had robbed me of speech.

The negation wave disintegrated all the Monty copies and punched into the white runes surrounding Monty's body. He bounced off the barrier and fell to his knees, gasping.

TK stood with her hands on her hips. "Are you warmed up now?"

"Quite warm, thank you."

"Good. Your skill has grown considerably since the Sanctuary, but this whole exercise is to help you understand the limitation of power and the respect it commands. You attempted to tether a Smith Bridge to me."

"I did, yes."

She moved a hand, and the air coalesced around Monty, turning to stone.

"That was a mistake."

The stone turned red and exploded. TK made a fist, and the fragments stopped midair. She turned her hand, opened it, and the barrage of stone rushed in at Monty.

He gestured, superheating the air around him. The fragments burst or turned to small pools of liquid around him, solidifying seconds later.

"Yes. Yes, it was."

Monty was looking a little worse for wear. Then I understood TK's strategy. She was wearing him down with large attacks, keeping him on the defensive as Monty had to keep countering.

What I didn't understand was why he was getting so tired so soon? It wasn't like him to fatigue this early in a fight.

"I'm glad you have clarity on the matter." TK extended an arm and formed a long black blade. I recognized it from the small statue in the Hall of the Ten. She advanced and slashed horizontally.

Monty dodged back. The blade cut though his suit jacket cleanly, leaving a long slice through the runically enhanced dragonscale. Monty looked down and poked a finger through the gash while raising an eyebrow.

A black orb punched him in the chest. He rotated with the blow, gesturing and forming a wall with the sand on the floor. Another orb punched through the pink wall of sand. He raised an arm and absorbed the impact with a sickening crunch, backpedaling to the edge of the combat area.

He gestured and sent a white orb aimed at TK's head. She stood still and raised a hand. The blast stopped several inches from her face. She slapped the orb with a backhand and returned it to Monty faster than my eyes could track. It exploded with a bright flash upon contact.

Monty slid across the floor. His suit was in tatters. His face was covered in cuts and bruises. The arm he had used to absorb the impact of the orb looked broken. He stood shakily for a few seconds before falling to one knee.

TK walked over and placed the tip of her blade

beneath Monty's chin. She whispered something I couldn't make out. He stiffened, slowly stood, and gave her a nod. She returned the nod, the blade disappeared, and she turned to the dais.

"This Reckoning is complete to my satisfaction." TK's voice echoed the same way Dahvina's had, as she approached the dais. "The conditions of blood and power have been met."

Dahvina stood, stepped forward, and gestured. My arms dropped to my side as the barrier fell around the combat area. The violet glow in the pendant became a faint glimmer. I placed it under my shirt again and stretched my sore shoulders.

"Shieldbearers, attend to your mages," Dahvina said, motioning to the Wordweavers. I approached Monty.

"You look wrecked," I said under my breath as we walked to the center of the floor. "I mean that in a good way."

"She was holding back the whole time. I grossly miscalculated the extent of her power. It was foolish and arrogant of me to think I could tether a Smith Bridge to her."

I glanced over at TK, who spoke quietly with LD. She looked like she had just gone for a walk, not been in a battle of mages. Monty, on the other hand, looked like he had been chewed up and spit out by Planet Peaches.

"She was... holding back?"

Monty nodded and winced. "For all my talk of

her volatility, she demonstrated an incredible degree of self-restraint during the Reckoning."

We stood in the center of the combat area.

"I consider this matter settled." Dahvina looked at us and then turned to face the members of the dais. "There will be no further action taken on the events of today."

All the members of the dais nodded. Dahvina turned to us. "Blood and power have been reckoned. The outcome has been determined. Do you both agree?"

TK and Monty both nodded.

"Let the shieldbearers be witnesses to this Reckoning."

LD bowed and nudged me again to copy him.

"We bear witness."

Two Wordweavers stepped next to Monty and escorted him out of the combat area. Mahnes disappeared, and Kristman Dos went over to have words with Jimmy the Butcher, probably to discuss Were matters.

Badb walked over to Dex, who kept a wary eye on her as she approached. I saw Michiko disappear from the rear of the dais and appear a few seconds later on the lower level.

She walked over to me, and my heart did that strange flip-flop beat it always did when I saw her. Her black Chanel dress had a long slit, that revealed one leg. A large red dragon design coiled itself around her body, the head starting at her shoulder and the tail peeking out by her thigh. Her piercing eyes fixed me in place, and I had to remember to breathe.

"Hello, Chi. It's good to see you."

"Simon, I'm pleased to see you survived London and the mage's home."

"Yes. Me, too." My power of wit and conversation knew no equal. "We just got back recently."

"I know. I can't stay. There is a situation in the Council. Something you need to look into."

"In the Council? Sure you don't want Ramirez and the NYTF?"

The New York Task Force, or NYTF, was a quasi-military police force, created to deal with any supernatural event occurring in New York City. They were paid to deal with the things that couldn't be explained to the general public without causing mass hysteria.

They were led by Angel Ramirez, who was one of the best directors the NYTF had ever had.

"No, this is beyond his scope. Erik suggested we get you involved."

"Is this about Kokoutan no ken?"

Monty had placed Kokoutan no ken, the dark blade that was the other half of my own Ebonsoul, with Hades for safekeeping from the Blood Hunters. Hades thought it was a good idea to give the sword that kept most of the Dark Council in check to Grey Stryder, one of the last

Night Wardens—and a powerful dark mage, according to Monty.

If I was being honest, it wasn't the sword that kept the Council in check. It was the vampire standing in front of me. Her ferocity, cunning, and ruthlessness made her a dangerous ally and a fearsome enemy. The fact that we had some kind of 'thing' happening only proved that I had suffered one too many blows to the head in my youth.

She led the Council with an iron determination and a keen mind. Anyone who rose to challenge her, as allowed by the Dark Council, soon found out why she was feared and respected. Usually in the last few seconds of their life.

"The sword is with a dark mage who roams the city streets at night. If I need to recover it, I know where it is. No, this is about reports of activity near the Seaport."

"What? One of the ships drifted off to sea?"

She stared at me for a few seconds. "Does anyone consider you funny?"

"Plenty of people, I just haven't met them yet."

She nodded. "There have been large spikes in energy in the area. Erik thought it would be best if you looked into it *without* alerting the NYTF."

"Any idea what kind of spikes?"

"Yes. I need you to confirm or disprove my observations."

"As soon as we get back, we'll check it out."

Ramirez had left me messages about strange activity downtown near the South Street Seaport. Now Chi, along with Erik from the Hellfire Club, was mentioning the same thing. I didn't like the timing, especially with George out hunting dragons.

I didn't say anything to Chi about dragons, mostly because the last time we had faced a dragon we'd lost Lieutenant Cassandra Rott, an NYTF officer and George's daughter. He'd taken her death hard and held me partly responsible. Part of me felt he was right.

The last time George and I had spoken, he had mentioned finding dragons. Oh, and revenge. He definitely had a large case of revenge going on.

"They're going to pay for taking my little girl, and you're going to help me—you owe me, Strong. She died on your watch. You owe me, and you owe her."

I did owe him, several times over. I would have never made it through Shadow Company without George, but the idea of a dragon vendetta sounded completely suicidal.

"Be careful." Chi touched my cheek and disappeared.

We needed to get back right away.

SIX

MOST OF THE Triad members and Wordweavers were gone. Only TK, LD, Kristman Dos, Dex, Monty, and I remained in Fordey Boutique. I hadn't noticed when Badb left, but part of me was glad she'd decided on a stealthy exit.

<Can I have some meat now? No one dropped meat during the fight.>

<I told you no one was going to drop meat. Go ask Dex. Don't break him.>

Peaches padded over to Dex and nudged him, nearly knocking him down.

"Ach, hound!" Dex looked down at Peaches, who proceeded to unleash a large dose of hungry puppy-dog eyes.

<I heard this face is very effective in getting larger portions of meat.>

<Who told you that?>

<The bird with the light eyes.>

<Herk? You can speak to Herk?>

I lost his attention once Dex materialized two industrial-sized sausages, each the length of my arm. Peaches proceeded to inhale them as Dex placed them on the floor.

<See? It works.>

"Lad," Dex said, looking at me, "you're going to have to learn to make meat for your hound. It's an easy spell. You should have more success than you had with your orb of light."

LD chuckled. "You should get TK to show you. She knows how to make the never-ending one. If your hound eats slowly enough, he can have sausage for days."

Monty and TK were speaking off to one side. I was about to approach with the news Chi had given me, when Dex cleared his throat.

"How long?" Dex looked at LD and Kristman Dos.

"Two months, three at the outside," Kristman Dos answered. His deep voice resonated in the Danger Room. "I have reports of entire families disappearing up and down the seaboard. Every time I get close, nothing."

"How many of the Ten are you mobilizing?"

"LD, TK, and RJ to get us there."

"She got her Strix?"

Kristman Dos nodded. "She's very happy and says thank you. Oh, and the next time you hold an orb class in her plane, she's going to rip you a new one."

Dex laughed. "I got her a plane, didn't I?" He grew serious. "Can you give me a month? I have to head over to the Sanctuary and have a conversation with the remaining Elders and Ziller."

"A month is fine. We'll start up north and work our way down with the streak. Whatever is doing this is masking well."

"Well enough to avoid you?" LD asked. "Even in your other form?"

"In every form."

"I'd better pack heavy, then. Dex, give me a hand. Some of these items are volatile."

"If you hear an explosion, it'll mean LD screwed up," Dex said, trailing behind him.

LD left the Danger Room with Dex. Kristman Dos stared at me for a few seconds, then looked down at Peaches.

"You're bound to a hellhound?"

"His name is Peaches. You're really a weretiger?"

<He smells different.>

<He can turn into a big cat. Do not make him angry.>

<Do you think he has meat? Do cats like meat?>

<They do. Let's not ask him.>

Kristman smiled at my response. "Dex told me you had spirit." He glanced over to where TK and Monty were still speaking quietly. "You did well as a shieldbearer today. Usually a Reckoning sends the shieldbearer to the infirmary. You're stronger than you look."

"Thank you, I think."

"Did your mage friend really try to tether a Smith Bridge to TK?"

"It was one of his more suicidal ideas, but yes, he tried."

"Amazing," he said, mostly to himself. "Either TK really likes him, or she's mellowing out."

"What's so amazing?"

"That he's still alive. How long have you and the vampire been an item?"

"Item? We aren't an *item*." I looked around quickly to make sure Chi was gone. "It's complicated."

Kristman chuckled. "Relationships with them usually are."

"How did you know?"

He tapped the side of his nose. "You smell."

"Excuse me, I what?"

"No, not like that," he said with a smile. "Vampires, like my kind, leave their scent on those they've mated with. She's marked you as hers."

"Marked me? Wait…mated?"

How did she manage to leave her scent on me? When did she do this? It could explain a few things, like how she was always able to track my location. I'd have to ask her about this the next time we spoke. Or maybe have Dex do it and save myself the evisceration.

"You aren't mates?"

We had definitely crossed into the land of too

much information, bordered on one side by the river of awkwardness, and settled by the citizens of shame and embarrassment.

"Mates? No, not really. Like I said, it's complicated."

"You didn't know she marked you?" Kristman asked. "You have a large 'KEEP AWAY' sign over your head at all times for human and supernatural alike. I wouldn't count on any dates in your future."

I thought about the last date I'd been on with Katja and shuddered.

"My last date didn't go so well."

"I'm not surprised," he said with a sniff. "Your vampire is ancient and powerful. A vampire like that rarely joins with a human."

"I'm special that way." I rubbed Peaches' head. "At least, according to Monty."

Kristman appraised me with a long look that extended several seconds into creepy. His orange eyes gave off a faint glow and gave me the impression he was looking past me. After a few seconds more, he caught himself and shook his head.

"Forgive me for staring, I sometimes forget my manners when dealing with humans."

I figured it was a weretiger thing. I raised a hand and waved his words away. "It's not a prob—"

"Then again, you aren't exactly human, are you?"

I froze, and remembered Monty's look earlier when I'd almost shared I was immortal.

"No," Monty said, stepping next to me and pulling me away by the arm. "On occasion, even I wonder what planet he comes from. Would you excuse us?"

We stepped away. I glanced over my shoulder to see Kristman Dos staring at me, until TK interrupted his line of sight and diverted his attention by speaking to him.

"I think he knows about my extended life expectancy."

"Unlikely it's that specific. It's possible he senses something off about your energy signature."

"Like my incredible charisma and dazzling wit?"

"Those traits are not discernable with his senses, despite the illusion that you possess either. He would rely on his weretiger capabilities."

I nodded. "Said I smelled, wasn't exactly human, and that I'm Chi's mate, since she marked me."

"I suspected as much," Monty said, rubbing his chin. "It would explain quite a bit. We can investigate that further at another time."

"I don't know if I've just been insulted or complimented."

"Take it as a compliment." Monty brushed some hair out of his face. "Weretigers rarely communicate outside of their species or close friends. I think we may have a situation."

Anytime a mage said there's a situation, my first reaction was to run in the other direction. Situations, like conversations, usually meant pain, agony, and many angry creatures trying to shred me. That was a best-case scenario.

"Is that what you were discussing with TK?"

"What? No." He looked over to where TK stood. "She requested I keep watch over Fordey while they're out."

"You agreed? How do you watch a place that has no apparent fixed dimensions?"

"Carefully," he said, shaking his head. "Of course, I agreed. She just refrained from disintegrating me. I felt it was the least I could do, considering the outcome of the Reckoning."

"Which, I must say, you're looking less wrecked. The Wordweavers did a good job patching you up. What's the situation?"

"There have been energy spikes in lower Manhattan, near the Hellfire."

"I know." I shared what Chi had told me earlier. "Are energy spikes a problem?"

"Not usually, but this may be connected with your friend, Mr. Rott, and his recent fixation."

"It's not a fixation. George has a singular determination and will. When he sets his mind to something, it's a scary and fantastic thing to see."

"His *determination* may get us all killed."

"George said he found the dragons. That doesn't sound good. He was never all there, even back when he was in the NYTF. We all thought he hovered near the edge of sanity. Now, with Cassandra gone, I think he may have stepped over that edge into an abyss."

"I need to speak to my uncle before we go to Hybrid."

Monty turned and gave TK a nod, which she returned.

"I'll call Castor shortly," TK said, interrupting her conversation with Kristman Dos. "If anyone knows about this, he does. Or knows someone who does."

"Thank you," Monty said with a short bow.

Kristman Dos gave us a short nod and returned to the conversation he was having with TK.

We left the Danger Room and headed down the corridors of Fordey. Every few intersections, Monty would stop, gesture, and then read a section of the wall.

"Hybrid?" I asked, confused. "What hybrid? More importantly, is this *hybrid* going to attempt to chew our faces off?"

"Hybrid is a place, not a creature. If I recall, your time in the NYTF was as a member of a deep-cover black ops group. How long were you a part of Shadow Company?"

"My service in the NYTF was expunged from all records. That information is beyond classified."

"I know. I also know where to look. How well did you know George?"

"No one knew him well. We were all crazy, but George, he was the craziest. How bad are these energy spikes?"

"It's worse than you think."

"George Rott with revenge on the brain. I'm thinking that's pretty bad. He has resources and knows how to deal with supernatural threats. Don't see much worse than that."

Monty gestured, read the symbols on the wall of an intersection, and paused, looking at me. "A demigod may be involved."

"A what?"

"Demigod. Half human and half god. Is this a new concept for you?"

"No. I mean, I haven't met any...you mean like Hercules and Perseus?"

"That's just one pantheon. Every pantheon has demigods, most of them not as famous as those two."

"What do you mean 'involved?'"

"It's possible that the spikes are being caused—not by dragons, but by a demigod."

"Okay, that's worse."

"We need to go see the twins."

SEVEN

WE ARRIVED AT a large storage room. I marveled at how many corridors and rooms made up Fordey Boutique. Dex and LD were packing items into two large duffel bags.

"René better not give me shit, I got her a new plane," Dex growled, placing some items in one of the bags. "Well, technically Division 13 did, but you know what I mean."

"Technically, *you're* the reason she needed a new plane, you and your impromptu orb class." LD passed Dex a handful of small vials. "Can't believe you still speak to Division 13. Who did you call?"

Dex gave him a look and raised an eyebrow. "If I tell you, I'm going to have to silence you."

LD stared hard at Dex, who returned the stare with equal intensity for several seconds before they both burst into laughter.

"That was a good one, *pendejo*. Straight face and

everything. How are Luna and Reese?"

"Just saw Reese. Same as always." Dex was still chuckling when he turned to look at us. "Hello, Nephew. You're looking grim, as usual."

I glanced over at Monty, who scowled and pushed some hair from his face. "We have a situation, uncle."

"Whoa, Dex." LD crouched down to get some more items from a bottom shelf. "It's a *situation*. Glad we never faced one of those. This sounds serious."

Dex smiled and crossed his arms. "Don't tease. My nephew doesn't have a sense of humor. He lost it in a tragic accident at a young age."

"Really?" LD asked. "What happened?"

"Puberty." Dex gave Monty a huge grin. "He never recovered."

I suppressed a laugh and looked away, suddenly finding the ceiling of the storage room to be incredibly interesting.

Monty sighed and pinched the bridge of his nose. "There may be an enclave of dragons in the city."

"Shit!" LD said and banged his head on a shelf. "Are you serious?"

"I'm always serious. Did that sound humorous?"

"He never jokes," I confirmed with a shake of my head. "At least not on purpose."

Dex's face grew dark. "What else? There's more, isn't there?"

Monty paused and then spoke. "It's possible a demigod is involved."

Dex let out a string of words I figured were curses. Except they were curses I'd never heard. All I could make out were plenty of 'orts.'

"Any evidence of either? Demigod or dragon?"

"We're heading to Hybrid to speak to the twins. They may have information. TK is making the call."

"Good, be careful with those two. Avoid Pollux the Prick. Speak to Castor."

LD whistled low. "Dragons are nasty business, but dragons *and* demigods? Does TK know?"

Monty nodded. "Erik gave her most of the information before the Reckoning. She brought me up to speed after we, well, after she…"

"Trounced you soundly," Dex replied. "No shame in it, boy. You faced a superior opponent and still live to tell the tale. Well done. Your father would be been proud."

"Yes, after she defeated me," Monty answered quietly. "I still have much to learn, it seems."

"She didn't *defeat* you." LD approached, putting a hand on Monty's shoulder and shaking his head. "She kicked your ass six ways to Sunday. Don't feel bad. You weren't the first, and you won't be the last. Anyway, humble pie is good for the soul."

"I'd go with you, Nephew, but I'm due at the Sanctuary tomorrow," Dex said with a scowl. "The Elders gave me an extra day to attend the

Reckoning."

"You mean you had to ask *permission*?" LD asked. "Do you need me to write you an official Reckoning note?"

"Keep it up and there'll be another Reckoning today."

LD laughed and went back to searching the shelves for items. Dex turned to us, serious. He gestured and made a string of linked sausage. When he let them go, they floated to the other side of the room.

Peaches, riveted by the floating feast, followed them.

"LD is right. Dragons are a nasty business best dealt with by others. Do you want me to make a call?"

"No." Monty looked away. "We can handle it."

Dex raised an eyebrow and stepped close to Monty.

"You two and the hellhound can handle a dragon?"

"We have faced their kind in the past."

"You faced *one* dragon, lost a member of your team, and barely walked away from the encounter."

I remembered our encounter with Slif. She was an ancient dragon, working to undo the spread of magic among non-dragonkind. From what I'd surmised, they had a real problem with non-dragons using or having access to magic. If Dex knew about our fight with Slif, he was better informed than I realized.

"We didn't know she was a dragon," I said. "She fooled us all."

"That's my point, boy. You won't see them until they want to be seen. They can mask better than any mage, living or dead."

"I'm not walking away from this, Uncle."

"A man must do what he feels is right." Dex sighed and sounded very Monty-like. I wondered if this was a family trait. "Your head is thicker than your father's."

"Thank you," Monty said quietly. "I promise to contact you if we find an enclave."

"That's all I ask, lad. You've nothing to prove, not to me." Dex rested both hands on Monty's shoulders. "Don't make this personal. If you run across an enclave, call me, the Council, and the NYTF."

"And the demigod?"

"Aye, if a demigod is involved," Dex said, his voice steel, "I'll make the call."

EIGHT

MONTY GESTURED AND closed the rift behind us as we stepped into our office. I pulled out my phone and called Ramirez on his direct line.

"This'd better be a wrong number, Strong. I've had enough disasters to deal with today, much less whatever you're going to say to add to the long list."

"Rottweiler."

"Shit, not on the phone. Meet me where he lost his only love. One hour."

I hung up.

"Ramirez doesn't strike me as the cloak-and-dagger type. Why is he being so cryptic?" Monty made his way to the kitchen. "What does a man like George Rott love?"

"Not just love, his *only* love. Where he lost his only love." I tapped my chin. "The only thing George loved more than the job was his daughter

—Cassandra."

"Cassandra. Yes, that makes sense. If Ramirez wants to meet where Mr. Rott lost his love he means—?"

"Haven. He wants to meet at Haven."

"That would be less than ideal, considering the current circumstances. I'd rather we refrain from using Haven as a meeting place."

TK's words to Monty came back to me: *Your closest friend is cursed by Kali, you seem to be allergic to intact buildings, and you're in love with a hunted sorceress.*

"Who's hunting Roxanne and why?"

"She's warded, as is Haven. No one and nothing can get close to her while I'm alive. Call Ramirez and change the location."

"That wasn't my question," I said. "Is this classified mage information?"

"It's...difficult to explain," he answered and sipped his tea. "It's not classified, but telling you would put you in danger."

"Sounds classified to me," I said, dialing Ramirez again.

"What? I told you not over the phone," Ramirez barked. "Was my clue too difficult?"

"Please, Angel, that was amateur hour. Monty requested a different location."

"Really, did he give you a reason why?"

"He did," I said, looking over at Monty. "Let's do the Rump."

"You seem to have a fixation with this Rump.

Are you sure there isn't something you want to share?"

I could imagine the smile crossing his face.

"It's a meat shop."

"Sure, it is. I'm sure they have all kinds of *meat* there too." A chuckle escaped him. "Fine. See you there."

He hung up.

I shook my head. "That better?"

"Much. We can utilize the back room and make sure the conversation is secure."

"Then you can tell me why Roxanne is being hunted."

"Of course, what would be another group hunting you?"

"Hunting me? What are you talking about?"

"We've managed to anger dragons, trolls, and an entire group of European magic-users. The latter a result of the renovation of their meeting space by destroying the Tate Modern."

"That building needed demolishing, trust me."

"Not to mention the Blood Hunters, who are now being led by Esti. She appeared quite psychotic, and eager to introduce you to the business end of her knives in the pursuit of their dark blades. Shall I continue?"

"No, thanks." I held my hand up. "I need a cup of coffee."

"I'm not keeping secrets, Simon. This information is volatile. If I share it, it has the potential to attract the wrong attention. Attention we can ill afford at this moment."

"I get it. I'm just not looking forward to meeting any more dragons. Much less with demigods sprinkled on top."

"Neither am I," Monty admitted. "Let's meet with Ramirez, and then we'll head over to Hybrid and get more information."

"Can you call Cecil and get us another Goat? One that's magically meltproof?"

"I don't think 'magically meltproof' counts as a condition of his vehicles."

"You know what I mean, with super runes to protect it from melting spells like the last Goat."

"Super runes?" Monty raised an eyebrow. "Right. In any case, after London, he may be reluctant to give us a vehicle. But I can try."

"If we're going to be dealing with dragons, make sure it's fireproof too."

NINE

"WHAT DID CECIL say?"

We walked downstairs to the lobby of the Moscow. At Dex's insistence, Monty had arranged for the purchase of our space when we expanded the office.

After the purchase, I rarely saw Olga in the building. Her uncanny ability to always appear when the rent was due had never ceased to amaze me. I looked around the lobby, but she was nowhere in sight. After my encounter with Steigh Cea and her sisters, I was determined to ask Olga some subtle questions about the Jotnar. Andrei stood at the door, he stiffened and crossed himself, when he saw Peaches.

I was feeling particularly nice this afternoon.

<Go say hello to Andrei. He has meat for you.>

<Really? What kind?>

<What do you mean, what kind? Since when do you

care what kind of meat?>

<I don't smell any meat. Do I have to bite him? Is it magic meat?>

<Do not bite him. I'll get you meat at the Rump.>

<Bite his rump?>

<Don't bite him anywhere. Forget it. Just go outside.>

Peaches padded by Andrei, who crossed himself again and backed away from the door, whispering to himself.

"Andrei, can you tell Olga I'd like to speak to her?"

He nodded but kept his distance. "I tell Mrs. Etrechenko you want to talk."

"Thank you. Did you want to pet Peaches?"

"No! I mean no, thank you, Mr. Stronk. Very nice of you to offer, but no, thank you."

"Okay, if you change your mind, let me know."

Andrei shook his head and closed the door just a little faster than usual behind us. We stepped outside onto the empty sidewalk and into the afternoon sun. The valet wasn't waiting for us, since we were Goatless.

"Why do you insist on torturing him?"

"It's not torture. I'm helping Andrei grow by encouraging him to face his fears."

"Oh, this is character building? I thought you were just trying to scare him witless every time your creature walked past."

"C'mon, Monty, you know me. Would I do something like that to poor Andrei?"

"I'm going to assume that's a rhetorical question. Let's go. Cecil will deliver the new vehicle to the Rump."

"Is it a Goat? Tell me it's a Goat."

"He wouldn't say."

"Is it magically meltproof?"

"I informed him of your request for it to be covered in super runes and be magically meltproof."

"And?"

"He assured me that it would last longer than the Lamborghini Urus he loaned us in London, provided we don't strap a magical melting bomb to its chassis."

"He sounds upset. Did you explain that we didn't destroy the last Goat or the Urus? That it wasn't our fault?"

He nodded as we crossed the street. People usually gave us a wide berth when we walked on the block. Most of that was the reaction to Peaches.

"His response was, and I quote: 'Things have a way of blowing up around you two. Buildings and cars especially. I'm sure you had nothing to do with it, other than being in proximity.' End quote."

"You two? What does he mean you two? Most of the destruction is the result of your spells or one of your friends."

"And yet, it's surprising how many of our destructive episodes involve your presence.

Coincidence? Unlikely."

"Unlikely? I'm not the one dealing with magical forces." I moved my fingers to mimic his gestures. "All that destruction is you and your casting."

"Except for the Strix. That was all you."

"*That* was your insane uncle getting me to create an orb in a pressurized environment."

"In any case, Cecil requested I purchase this vehicle. This isn't a loaner from SuNaTran. I used the agency account, so we own whatever it is he's sending over."

"Wonderful," I groaned. "With our luck it'll be a Prius or a Gremlin."

"As long as it's magically meltproof," Monty said. "With super runes, of course."

I glared at him. It was a solid three on my glare-o-meter. He didn't flinch.

"Your sense of humor knows no bounds. Maybe you can start a mage comedy group with your uncle?"

The Randy Rump was a block away from the Moscow and stayed open all night, only closing for a few hours in the early morning. It catered to the early evening and nighttime clientele—which was most of the supernatural community. The Rump had also become a popular meeting place since the Dark Council had declared its neutral status. It had gone from "butcher shop" to "butcher shop, restaurant, and meeting hall" in a few short weeks.

Jimmy stood behind the counter and gave me a

nod as he took care of some customers. His long gray hair was pulled back in a ponytail. He wore an apron over a dress shirt with the sleeves rolled up. It was the suit he had on during the Reckoning. His massive arms, which were easily the size of my legs, were covered with thick hair.

I looked around and realized that he had redone the seating area again. What used to be a single display case was now a set of two display cases, and the counter had been redone in marble and had been extended.

Tables and chairs filled the remaining floor space. Even in the middle of the afternoon, most of the tables were occupied with patrons who were eating and drinking.

Jimmy finished with the customer and came out from behind the counter. He had hired some help, and they took over serving the line while he stepped away. He wiped his hands on his apron, and motioned for us to follow him into his office.

A few of the patrons gave us looks as we followed Jimmy to the back. Most of them were focused on Monty and Peaches. They could tell he was a powerful magic-user, and Peaches, from what Monty told me, was covered in runes, even though I still couldn't see most of them.

Jimmy opened the door and let us enter first. A few seconds later, one of his employees came in with a large titanium bowl filled with meat. Peaches was one of Jimmy's favorite customers.

"I got him a new bowl." Jimmy looked down at the slobbering black hole that was my hellhound. "This one is a Grade five titanium alloy. Should be Peaches-proof."

The employee gave Jimmy the bowl and backed out of the office, keeping a wary eye on Peaches as he did so. Jimmy put the bowl on the floor next to his desk. I saw the bowl contained some excellent cuts of meat and large sausages.

"You need to stop spoiling him. He's going to get fat."

"He's a hellhound." Jimmy rubbed Peaches' head. "He needs to keep his strength up."

<This place is almost as good as the other place.>

<If you keep eating like that, you won't be able to move when you need to. I'm going to put you on a diet.>

<A diet? That sounds like die. I don't like that word.>

<It just means having some control over how much you eat. You can't just eat all the meat.>

<Why not? It would be bad not to eat all the meat. Meat is life.>

He proceeded to bury his face in the bowl and devour the meal.

"Keep his strength up? Does he look weak or sickly to you?"

"No, he doesn't," Jimmy answered, rubbing Peaches' flanks. "And we're going to make sure he stays large and strong."

I never worried about Jimmy keeping his arms attached to his body with Peaches. My hellhound was smart enough not to shred the hands that fed him. It also helped that Jimmy was a werebear, and I was sure, on some level, Peaches smelled or sensed the animal in him. The black hole known as Peaches inhaled the meat in seconds.

"You've made some changes," I said, looking around at the new office.

"The last one didn't survive your last visit, so I figured I'd make some changes to the space with the renovations. You're not expecting any violent friends…are you?"

"I only have one violent friend." I glanced over at Monty, who pointed at Peaches. "Well, two."

"It's just that every time you visit…"

"That was *one* time. That wasn't even us."

"Anyway… this is the new office." Jimmy motioned with one large hand, Vanna White style. "I'd like it to stay this way, if possible."

A large desk sat against the far wall, opposite the door. To the right of the desk and along the wall sat a large brown sofa. On the other side of the desk, against the left wall, I saw two tall, black filing cabinets.

His desk was neat, with several piles of papers in organized stacks along the surface. An industrial-sized computer monitor took up almost half the desk.

Even though the office was spacious, it still felt slightly cramped because Jimmy was just this side of enormous. I wondered if all werebears were on the large size. He was the only one I knew. He sat in the chair behind the desk and leaned back.

On the back wall, I noticed something else.

"That's new." I pointed to a wooden door.

"I had it installed recently with the last of the renovations," Jimmy answered. "I didn't want to open the main door every time we needed the backroom."

"Is Ramirez here yet?"

"He got here about five minutes ago. He's inside waiting for you. You can go through there."

The door was a smaller version of the main door in the butcher shop securing the entrance to the backroom. The door and frame were made of Australian Buloke ironwood. I narrowed my eyes and saw that it was magically inscribed with runes on every inch of its surface. It stood six feet tall and half as wide. I was sure Jimmy had to stoop to get in that way.

"This leads to the backroom?"

Jimmy nodded. "Same sequence too."

Monty gave Jimmy a short bow. "Thank you for being part of my Triad this morning. I do appreciate your response on such short notice."

Jimmy waved Monty's words away. "The honor was mine. I've never been to a Reckoning before. We settle things a little more violently in my sleuth. Whoever walks away, wins."

"I don't expect to experience another Reckoning in my lifetime." Monty stepped to the wooden door. "Same sequence, you said?"

Jimmy nodded. "After that Negomancer took the Rump apart, I thought you mages were dangerous. After seeing TK in action, whoa...she's scary *and* dangerous. I wouldn't want to face her, even in my other form."

"She is quite formidable." Monty nodded and pressed the runes on the door in sequence. "That should do it."

The door was over a foot thick. Opening it was surprisingly easy if you knew the rune sequence. If you didn't, you'd need the equivalent of a magical nuke, and that would probably just scratch the surface. Once closed, it remained closed. Period.

It swung open easily and I peeked inside. The backroom of the Rump was considerably smaller than the front area. It consisted of one large room with three tables. Two of them, placed along the north and south walls, were long and rectangular. The third table in the center, was round. Each of them had seating for seven. Each table was heavy, dark oak, inscribed with runes along their surface.

Ramirez sat at the large, round table. In front of him, I saw a folder and a large pot of coffee. The aroma of coffee filled my lungs and all of a sudden, everything was right with the world. Coffee had that effect on me. I searched the inside pockets of my jacket and found my flask.

"Would you like a London Fog, Tristan?" Jimmy asked. "One of my guys is English and swears it's amazing. I haven't had one myself."

"No, thank you. As enticing as that sounds, I'll take Earl Grey with lemon and steeped for four minutes, if you please."

"I'll have it brought in."

Ramirez looked up when we entered the backroom. I heard the door lock behind us. I turned and saw the runes in the door flare bright orange for a brief second.

I filled a cup with coffee, opened my flask, and poured in a spoonful of Valhalla Javambrosia. I brought the cup to my lips, closed my eyes, and took a moment to inhale the aroma. Only after enough of the fragrance had filled my lungs did I allow myself to take a long sip, savoring the absolute caffeine goodness. Ramirez stared at me throughout my process.

"You need help." Ramirez shook his head. "Clearly, you're not getting out enough."

"You think I'm bad? Wait four minutes and watch him drink tea," I said, pointing at Monty. "How are you, Angel?"

"How am I? How do you think I am? Stressed and dealing with more shit than I can handle."

"So, the usual then?"

He gave me a tight smile and a nod. "The usual, yeah."

"Are we good?" The last time we had spoken, really spoken, was when we had lost Lieutenant Cassandra. The conversation had been loud and angry, so was he.

Peaches padded over and plopped down on the floor near my feet with a chuff.

"Is your dog okay?" Ramirez looked down at Peaches warily. "Did you get him a new collar?"

"He just stuffed his face. He's good. What about us?"

He paused for a moment, rubbed his face, and took a sip of coffee from his cup. "We're good. This, however,"—he slid the folder across the table to me—"is not."

I opened the folder and saw a picture of George 'Rottweiler' Rott staring back at me.

TEN

THE PICTURE LOOKED recent.

"When was this picture taken?" I looked down into the aged face of George 'Rottweiler' Rott, one of the best black ops team leaders. Meticulous and flexible. His missions were still being studied in the NYTF academy.

"A few weeks ago." Ramirez took another sip. "He's gone underground. We haven't been able to locate him since."

"And you won't unless he wants you to."

"That's why I'm here talking to you."

I looked at the picture again. He still wore a screaming-eagle cut and the years were showing, not that I would tell him that to his face. The eyes were the same. Fierce, intense, and approaching insanity. The most dangerous individuals I'd faced were those who had nothing to lose. George had the look of someone who had lost it all.

I flipped through the pages of the file. Many of them had redacted sections. In fact, most of them were redacted. I looked through the dates; there was at least a decade of activity before I'd joined. Shadow Company had been busy doing things best kept secret.

"Not much info here." I pointed to the file. "Most of this has been purged or expunged. Pretty useless."

"Turn to the back." Ramirez motioned with a hand. "I think you'll find something useful there."

"You and your cryptic comments. You should've been a spy."

"I missed my calling."

I flipped the pages and saw another, thinner file. This file was stamped RED—Retired Extremely Dangerous.

It was my file.

There was one page. A picture of a younger me from my Company days and a list of dates with redacted information next to each entry.

"Where did you get this?" I held up the sheet. "This isn't supposed to exist."

Ramirez nodded and took another sip of coffee.

"May I?" Monty held out a hand. I passed him the sheet. He began scanning it. "If you combine the two files, you can glean a good amount of information on Simon's past, with his file acting as the key, providing the dates for cross reference."

"That's the only copy anywhere, and it was a

bitch to get a hold of," Ramirez said. "I wasn't specifically looking for Strong's info, it just came attached with Rott's"

"Where did you get it?" I asked. "That information isn't supposed to be documented. Period."

"Like I told you, I've been doing some research in my spare time."

"Spare time?" I asked, incredulous. "Since when do you have spare time?"

"Ever since I lost a lieutenant to a dragon."

The words hung in the air between us for a few seconds.

"Shit, Angel…"

He held up a hand and shook his head. "I said we're good. But he isn't." He pointed at George's picture. "Lieutenant Cassandra went down in the line of duty. She knew the risks, we all do. Doesn't make it any easier for any of us, but he's not coming at this like an officer. He's dealing with this as a father who lost his only child. *That* makes him dangerous and volatile."

"I don't know why she was out there. She was good, but she wasn't NYTF ready." I shook my head, remembering Cassandra's adaptation period. The NYTF was trained to deal with the supernatural. They had extensive psych evals to help them cope with things they encountered that were supposed to be impossible.

Because of George's influence, Cassandra

bypassed all of that and went into the field unprepared. If the dragon hadn't ended her, it was only a matter time before something else just as lethal had. George, the black ops leader, knew this, but George, the father, could never accept that.

Ramirez reached into a bag and pulled out another file. "This file doesn't exist. You never saw it."

Monty put down my sheet and raised an eyebrow at the new file.

"Whose is it?" I asked.

"When we started getting energy spikes downtown, I assigned Jhon and his crew to measure the spikes' origin points."

"What did they find?" Monty asked. "Were they able to determine the nature of the energy?"

"I asked them to measure the spikes and to make note of any persons of interest." Ramirez slid the file to me. "They came back with this."

I opened the file and my blood froze. I looked into the tan face of a young man in his mid-twenties. A riot of black hair that had never seen a brush covered his head. It was the eyes that stopped me, though. I had seen eyes like that before. If George was approaching insanity, whoever this was had embraced it and wore it like a favorite suit.

I slid the file over to Monty in silence. He looked at the picture and flexed his jaw. I felt the shift in energy immediately.

"You two know who this is?" Ramirez asked, pointing at the picture. "If you do, I need that information. I lost four men getting this."

"I don't know who that is, but I recognize the eyes."

Monty nodded and sipped his tea. "Would it be possible to keep this photo?"

"Normally I'd say no, but I have nothing on this guy. No databases, not even facial recognition." Ramirez rubbed his face. "Go ahead. On the condition that any info you get comes to me first."

Monty took the photo and placed it in front of him on the table next to my file sheet.

"I'll make sure Simon keeps you informed."

"What were you saying about the eyes, Strong?"

I took a long pull of coffee. "The last time I saw eyes that off, I was facing an angry goddess."

"An angry what?"

"Kali, the Hindu goddess of death and violence," I said quietly. "Your guy has the same eyes."

"Well, shit. Is this guy a god?"

"Don't know. I hope not. That would truly suck if he's the one responsible for Jhon's team. Gods are hard to apprehend."

"Wow, no wonder you're a detective." Ramirez stared at me. "That observation was *amazing*."

"All of a sudden, everyone has a sense of humor." I put my cup down. "If he's a god, I hope you know the NYTF won't be able to deal with him."

"Leave that to me. We have a few things in R&D."

"A few things in R&D? Are you kidding? You have something that can stop a god?"

"Like I said, you call me when you find out anything about Crazy Eyes or George."

Ramirez grabbed his bag and put the files away. He held his hand out for the sheet from my file. Monty began handing it over when it burst into flame, turning to ash seconds later.

"My apologies, Director. Seeing the picture of that gentleman distracted me."

Ramirez glared. "Distracted *you*? I thought you magic-using wizards didn't get distracted?"

Monty narrowed his eyes and stared at Ramirez. "Wizards?"

I winced at the mention of wizards. I shook my head slowly. "Don't call him a wizard." I picked up the rest of the file and handed it to Ramirez. "Monty's a mage. Big difference."

"He's a sneaky bastard is what he is," Ramirez said under his breath, glaring at Monty. "I told you it was my only copy, and then he goes getting *distracted* and flames your file? That wasn't a distraction, that was intentional."

Ramirez took the remaining papers and shoved them into his bag. He pushed his chair back and stood to leave. "You find out who this guy is and locate George too. I have a feeling these two are connected somehow, and that can't be good."

I escorted Ramirez toward the main entrance. It opened a few seconds later as Jimmy poked his head in. I looked at him, surprised. He pointed at the corner with his chin.

"Cameras. After last time, no more surprises."

I looked to the corners and noticed the dim red lights in each one. "Smart move." I nodded in approval. "The director will be leaving."

"I'm not done doing research, Strong." Ramirez turned, giving me a scowl. "I need to know who or what I'm dealing with. Especially regarding this 'Shadow Company' you were in."

"You need to leave that alone, Angel, really. Let's focus on George and on stopping him before he does something that can get us all killed."

"I'm focusing on George *and* Shadow Company. Seems your group was a bit on the deranged side."

"Digging up my past will only give you nightmares."

"Nightmares? You two loose in my city is a waking nightmare every day. Besides, you can never outrun your past. It defines who you are, who you become."

"Very profound." I stepped closer to him so I could lower my voice. "If you keep digging into Shadow Company, you'll attract attention. The kind of attention you don't want. Leave it alone."

"I'm not scared of a little attention," he said under his breath and matching my tone. "I'll take my chances. Find George and the mystery man with the crazy eyes."

I paused for a few seconds. His trying to unearth my past was going to be a problem. I was going to have to call Hack."

"Top of the to-do list, promise." I was about to head back to the table when he grabbed my arm.

"Oh, and no more blown-up buildings. It's been quiet since you two have been out of the city. No major explosions, and my city has stayed in one piece. Let's keep it that way."

"Why does everyone look at me when they say that?" I removed my arm from his hand with a tug. "I'm not the one you need to be speaking to."

Ramirez pushed his way past Jimmy to exit the room. "Call me the moment you have something."

Jimmy didn't follow and waited until Ramirez had exited the Rump before approaching the table.

"Why is everyone blaming me for your destruction?" I said.

Monty looked up from the picture. "Possibly because you're at the scene of each instance of said destruction?"

"As are you," I replied. "Yet, I don't see anyone blaming you for blowing up their buildings. Since when does my being at the scene mean I'm the cause?"

"Most sane people refrain from accusing mages of anything. Something to do with wielding matter-altering energy."

"And mages being perpetually cranky."

"This is going to be a problem." Monty pointed at the picture of the man with the crazy eyes. "George is not capable of producing energy spikes on his own."

Jimmy cleared his throat with a cough. "There's someone outside waiting for you in the shop."

I looked at Monty. "You expecting someone?"

"Not particularly." He picked up the photo and put it in an inside pocket. "We should see who it is, though."

I made sure Grim Whisper and Ebonsoul were easily accessible and followed them out.

ELEVEN

THE RUNEWORK DEFENSES in the Randy Rump were some of the best. Considering it served as a neutral location, I expected very little magical activity inside its walls.

I narrowed my eyes and looked at the rune-covered columns. I noticed that the walls, floor, and ceiling were also covered in intricate symbols.

"You added runework to the defenses?"

"Yes," Jimmy answered and waved to one of the patrons. "One of the mages from the Council offered to reinforce them after your—last time. I like the place as a meeting hall and butcher shop, not a crater."

The Rump had a vibrant energy. I saw a few mages and assorted magic-users discussing theorems in animated conversations. Once or twice I heard the name Ziller. Others were intently studying thick books.

Not everyone in the Rump was a magic-user. The majority of the patrons were from the surrounding neighborhood, picking up choice cuts of meat for dinner or sitting down and enjoying an afternoon cup of coffee.

I counted six mage guards standing or sitting in strategic locations throughout the seating area. Once night fell, the mage guards would be replaced with vampires or shifters of some sort. The Dark Council took the safety and neutrality of its designated locations seriously. Violating the established rules of neutral locations could end in permanent retirement...from life. They were taking extra precautions with the Rump after Beck, a Negomancer, had decided to explode the place.

Jimmy led us to a corner of the Rump. It was a group of three tables, and all but one was empty. Seated there, alone, was a short, older man who radiated power. His broad frame took up most of the corner, and his rough callused hands were wrapped around a large flagon of yellowish liquid I didn't recognize. The smell coming from the flagon reminded me of honey.

Jimmy moved two tables and relocated some chairs for Monty and me. "He's making the guards nervous," he said under his breath. "Is this a friend of yours?"

I shook my head. "Never seen him before. I think he belongs to Monty's club of magic-users."

"He does." Monty pulled out a chair and moved

to sit at the table. "But he's not a magic-user in the traditional sense."

"What's he drinking?" I asked, looking at the industrial-sized flagon. "I don't recognize it."

"Mead," Jimmy said under his breath.

"Mead? As in honey-wine? You know how to make mead?"

"I do now. He gave me the recipe a while back. This particular blend is called Acerglyn," Jimmy answered and looked warily at the figure seated at the table. "Tristan, is your intense friend going to unleash anything that can destroy the Rump?"

"No," Monty answered, "he's just here to make a delivery. Isn't that right, Cecil?"

"Quite right." The air around him crackled with orange energy. Cecil rubbed a hand through his short gray hair, rubbed his neatly trimmed goatee, and gave Jimmy a tight smile. "Just a delivery."

"Right, in that case, I'll leave you to it. Make sure you keep any and all destructive energies localized in this"—Jimmy made a circular motion around the table with a hand—"general area. We just finished renovations." He finished by giving me a look and then walked away.

"Did you see that look?" I said, pulling up a chair. "Why is he looking at me?"

"No, sorry, I missed it," Monty replied, turning to Cecil. "Since when do you deliver anything? Where's Robert?"

"Robert's out and about, running some errands.

This vehicle needed some special attention, which is why I'm here."

"Cecil, this is Simon Strong. I don't think you've formally met."

"I know who he is, Tristan," Cecil said, giving me a short nod, which I returned. "Anyone who gets a SuNaTran vehicle gets vetted by my people. We know all about Mr. Strong."

The way he'd said that last sentence set off my radar. Maybe I was just anxious after my conversation with Ramirez, but it felt like Cecil knew more about me than I'd feel comfortable sharing.

"Tell me it's not a Prius, please." I looked outside but didn't see any vehicle. "What is it?"

"I'll get to that in a second." Cecil raised a hand, taking a long drink of the mead. The sweet smell grew stronger as he drank. "Ahh, haven't had mead this good in a long time. Ever since home. That Jimmy is an artist."

He looked off into the distance wistfully.

"Where exactly is home?"

"Nevermind." He waved my words away. "Let's discuss the reason I'm here. Your vehicle."

Cecil rested his elbows on the table, steepled his fingers, and looked at us in silence. I swore his hazel eyes flickered with power as they bored into me. I wondered how bad it was if it was taking him this long to tell us.

"Damn, it's a Gremlin, isn't it?" Cecil remained

silent. "God, worse than a Gremlin? Is it an AMC Pacer?"

"Tristan," Cecil said, breaking his silence, "you recall several years ago, we took a 1970 Chevy Camaro and created a SuNaTran vehicle?"

"I heard the rumors," Monty said, his voice grim. "You didn't bring us *that*, did you?"

Cecil shook his head. "No, that's being used by someone else."

Monty raised an eyebrow in surprise. "You allowed that vehicle out on the road?"

"The Beast is *cursed*, not evil."

"I heard three drivers died after driving it."

"Technically, that's true."

"Technically?" I stared at Cecil. "What kind of car kills its driver?"

"The cursed kind," Monty replied before Cecil could answer. "Something to do with the runic configuration and its disruption of life energies. What did you bring us?"

"Who is driving this Beast now?" I wondered aloud.

"That's not important," Cecil answered quickly. "What's important is that I was able to decipher some of the runes that made the Beast indestructible and apply them to your vehicle."

"You gave us a cursed vehicle?" I looked at Monty, who held up a hand and sighed. "Is he *trying* to kill us?"

Monty narrowed his eyes. "I know you're still

upset about London and the Urus. We can reimburse you for the cost and any difficulty you incurred. There's no need to foist a cursed vehicle on Simon."

"Wait, what do you mean 'on Simon'?"

"That's just it," Cecil added with a hint of excitement. "Mr. Strong is the perfect driver...if the rumors are true."

"What rumors?" I asked cautiously.

"That you can't die."

TWELVE

"WHERE DID YOU hear these *rumors*?" Monty sat back, but I could feel the shift in energy around the table. "I'm curious."

"Mostly my own research from previous incidents. I like to keep an eye on the people who drive my vehicles."

"You've been keeping tabs on us?"

"SuNaTran is my reputation, my name," Cecil answered, staring at me. "You can rest assured I keep track of my vehicles *and* their drivers, especially when SuNaTran vehicles are being melted or exploded."

"Those were...extenuating circumstances," Monty mumbled.

"Your 'extenuating circumstances' are making my vehicles look bad." Cecil pointed at Monty. "After watching you two for a while, I realized it wasn't my vehicles. It was the complete and total shitstorm you two generate around you."

"I wouldn't classify it as a 'shitstorm,' but there does seem to be an element of chaos that encompasses our activities whenever we—"

I shook my head. "It's a shitstorm, Monty. Between your spells and my investigative prowess —"

"Prowess? More like reckless abandon." Monty pinched the bridge of his nose. "Cecil, what did you learn in your observations?"

"Things that should've been fatal to Mr. Strong here, weren't." Cecil kept staring at me. It was starting to creep me out. He turned back to Monty. "Sure, he can take a beating and is reckless as hell. But there were situations he shouldn't have walked away from, *unless* he wasn't normal."

"I'm just lucky."

"No, this isn't luck." Cecil glanced at Peaches, who rumbled at him. "Also, there's been talk about an immortal detective with a large dog-like creature who"—he looked down at Peaches again —"happens to be the offspring of a certain mythological creature, and runs around with a mage partner. By the way, that's a nice collar. Who did the work?"

"Fordey Boutique," Monty said. "TK specifically."

Cecil nodded in admiration, staring at Peaches' collar. He didn't get closer because the rumble increased in volume as he leaned in.

"A regulator and temporal enhancer?" Cecil shifted in his seat to get a better look at the collar. "He's gone huge?"

"You've been to Nidavellir?" Monty asked.

"Not in ages. TK managed to reshape entropy stones?" He tugged on his goatee and appraised the collar with admiration. "I've always said that woman was skilled."

"Where is all this talk happening?" I looked at them, slightly confused about where the conversation was going. "That's what I'd like to know, and where is Nidavellir?"

Cecil turned to face me. "You three don't exactly blend in, and you've made some powerful enemies. Take the car. Calibrate to the runes, and call me if you experience any side effects."

"Side effects? Like sudden death?"

"Sure, or worse."

"Worse...than death?"

"There are plenty of things that are worse than death." Cecil reached into his coat pockets, clearly looking for something. "Here they are."

He stood and placed two keyrings on the table. Attached to each ring was a fob and what looked like a metal Bluetooth symbol.

"The new car has Bluetooth?"

Cecil glared at me with a 'how have you managed to live this long?' look and shook his head before turning to Monty. "Those are binding runes. Your new vehicle is camouflage capable.

Once you calibrate to it, and I suggest you both do, those runes will bind you to the car so you can locate it wherever it is. Think runic GPS. Try not to park it where someone will smash into it. It would be bad…for them."

"Can we both drive it?" Monty asked, picking up a keyring. "Or are the runes you deciphered the same ones that hold the curse?"

"I suggest you let Mr. Strong drive the car, as a precaution. Just until the kinks are worked out."

"You mean to see if the car will try and kill me."

"Something like that. Plus, you're going to help me with another little problem I have. Let's get you in your new vehicle. It's around the corner."

We followed Cecil outside. I saw Jimmy keeping an eye on us as we headed out of the Rump.

"Do these runes affect anyone else in the car?" Monty asked once we were outside. "Or is it only the driver?"

"Only the driver. It has to do with the defensive runic configuration around the vehicle. These particular runes have to be placed under the driver for the protective sphere to enclose the vehicle."

"Have you tried shifting the location?"

Cecil shook his head. "We tried. Placing it anywhere else causes the sphere to collapse in on itself." Cecil pointed ahead. "Over there."

I looked down the street and saw nothing.

"Where?"

Cecil reached into a pocket and pulled out a

small black box. It gleamed in the afternoon sun and reminded me of a large entropy stone. The box had several buttons on its surface, each covered with runes. He pressed a combination of buttons, and a vehicle shimmered into sight.

"There," he said with a smile. "That's your new car."

THIRTEEN

I LOOKED WHERE Cecil pointed, and my heart skipped a few beats. For a few seconds, it was difficult to breathe. A deep purple, almost black, 1967 Pontiac GTO cruise machine with tinted windows materialized in front of my eyes. The last time I'd seen it, a Ghost had killed it with a black orb of death.

"I'm still not driving that monstrosity," Monty said. "Once again, the steering wheel is on the wrong side, Cecil."

"It's a...it's a Goat," I half-whispered. "Can I?"

Cecil motioned for me to get closer.

The Pontiac GTO got its name from the Ferrari 250 GTO, a rare and beautiful piece of automotive art. The GTO stands for Grand Tourismo Omologato. I'm sure no one wanted to say that mouthful—so GTO became Goat, and a legendary muscle car was christened.

As much as I could appreciate Italian artisanship, nothing came close to American muscle. When it came to muscle cars, for me, the Goat rose above them all.

"How did you—?" I looked at Cecil. "It's a Goat."

"You *do* realize there were quite a few of them made, right? Thousands actually."

"Of course." I nodded. "I just thought after London you were going to give us a Pacer or a Pinto. You know, something horrendous to drive and be seen in as payback for the destruction of the Urus."

"No," Cecil said with a smile. "I made sure Tristan bought this one."

"Yes, the price was exorbitant. A grand total of one dollar."

I looked at Cecil. "Really?"

"I couldn't just give it to you. There's a principle involved."

"A whole dollar?"

"For this vehicle there had to be an exchange. A cost was needed."

"You needed to use agency funds, really?" I looked at Monty. "I hope that didn't shatter the account."

"I equipped it with everything the other one had plus a few extras, and if you manage to destroy this one, it will help me with the Beast."

"*That's* your real motivation," Monty said. "Your

'little problem' is that you don't know *how* to destroy the Beast."

"What does that have to do with the Goat?" I asked. "Why does he need to destroy the Beast?"

"Contrary to his assessment of 'cursed over evil,' the car is a danger to everyone but the driver, it seems."

"Why not blast it to small Beast pieces?"

"I've tried everything," Cecil said with a sigh. "The thing is indestructible."

"He's counting on us getting this vehicle destroyed." Monty looked at the new Goat. "And solve the issue he has with the abomination he created."

"You don't understand." Cecil held up a hand. "It's not like that at all."

"Tell me," Monty said, his voice low with an edge of menace. "How *exactly* is it?"

"You owe me," Cecil started. "Because of you two...SuNaTran's name, my name, is getting tarnished."

"Tarnished? Really?" Monty replied.

"Here's a request I received yesterday." Cecil pulled out his phone and scrolled through his text messages. "'Could you provide me with a vehicle? Preferably the non-exploding or melting model. Thank you.'"

"That's harsh," I said, suppressing a giggle as I turned away. "Funny...but harsh."

"I'm so glad this amuses you." Cecil held up the

phone and pointed at Monty. "I get more and more messages like this every day."

"And you want us to do what exactly?" Monty brushed some strands of hair out of his face.

"I need you to conduct your business using this car, showing the supernatural community that my cars will keep them safe. Not explode or melt on them."

"He does have a point," I said, composing myself. "We, meaning you, are the reason the cars seem unsafe."

Cecil nodded. "It has very little to do with the Beast." His face grew dark. "I don't think there's a way to destroy that thing."

"I'm still not driving it." Monty headed over to the passenger side. "We will discuss this later."

"It's keyed to have a primary and secondary driver, no valet driving," Cecil added with a nod. "If one of you isn't driving, it's not moving. Mr. Strong, you first."

"That seems shortsighted." I approached the Goat and placed my hand on the door handle. The entire car flared bright orange for several seconds. I saw runes race along its surface and slowly fade away. The metal binding rune in my hand turned to dust.

"Not shortsighted, safe." Cecil motioned to Monty. "Now you, Tristan."

Monty grabbed the handle on the passenger side and the same effects repeated themselves.

"Unlock it," Cecil said. "I've provided you with a SuNaTran emblem allowing for parking anywhere in the city. It's etched into the Lexan windshield."

I turned the handle and heard the familiar metal clang as the doors unlocked. Something that sounded like a hammer striking an anvil came from under the hood. An orange glow flashed over the Goat and faded slowly.

I opened the back door and Peaches bounded in, rocking the Goat and demonstrating his professional sprawling ability. The suicide doors were a nice touch. I was fairly certain 1967 Pontiac GTOs were standard with two doors. The added doors allowed Peaches easy access to his backseat sprawlfest.

<It could have been unsafe. You should wait until I turn it on.>

<Unsafe for who?>

I was about to answer when I realized it was a good question. What was unsafe for a hellhound?

I could see the smoke wafting up from the surface of the Goat. The color fluctuated from deep purple to black, leaning more to black.

"At least it's not a grape anymore. Thank you, I like this color better."

"Yes, it goes by the exotic name of…black. I tried painting it with the Byzantium." Cecil shook his head. "It burned most of it off. This is all that remained."

"Are you saying this is a Beast Goat now?" I

asked. "A zombie Goat? An Undying Goat?"

"Is he always this way?" Cecil asked Monty.

"Only when he's awake."

"One more: The Goat from Beyond?"

"Do you think you can just get in and start it, please?" Cecil asked, stepping away from the car. "Let me know if you feel anything odd."

I placed my hands on the wheel, and red runes came to life along the dashboard. They pulsed for thirty seconds and then disappeared. I held my breath and started making choking noises.

Cecil ran over to my side, his face full of concern. Monty slid into the passenger side and adjusted his seatbelt while I convulsed behind the wheel. I placed both hands around my neck and clawed at my throat, trying to catch a breath. Monty slowly examined the glove compartment.

"Are you okay?" Cecil asked worriedly, fumbling at my seatbelt, trying to get it loose. "What's wrong? Tristan, what's wrong with him?"

"There aren't enough hours in the day to explain what's wrong with him."

"No...no new car smell," I said and fell back in my seat with a gasp. "You couldn't spring for a pine tree?"

Cecil stopped pulling at my belt, clenched his hand into a fist, and for a brief second I thought he was going punch me in the face.

"That's not funny...not funny at all."

"I disagree. Ask Monty."

Cecil looked over to where Monty sat carefully ignoring me.

"Positively side-splitting." Monty closed the glove compartment. "I can barely contain myself from the hilarity."

Cecil glared at us. "There's something wrong with the both of you." He looked into the back seat and saw Peaches on his back in superior sprawl position taking up all the available space in his seat. "The three of you. Even your hound is mental."

"His name is Peaches," I said seriously. "Not *hound*, thank you very much."

"Peaches? Who names a hellhound Peaches?"

"That's his name, because—like a peach—he is soft, sweet, and slobbery."

"Thank you for the vehicle, Cecil," Monty said. "If anything should arise, like Simon's spontaneous demise, I'll make sure to give you a call."

I adjusted my seatbelt. I placed a finger on the dash panel near the steering wheel. The engine roared and settled into a purr, vibrating in my gut. I closed my eyes and basked in the sensation and sound for a few seconds.

"The runic biometrics are a nice touch." I opened my eyes. "Really, thank you, Big C. If we explode, melt, or otherwise trash this wonderful vehicle, you'll be the first person I call."

"Big C?" Cecil stepped back. "Where are you going?"

"The Hybrid."

"The Hybrid? Have you grown tired of living? Neither of you are demigods. That place is suicide for you."

"We need to go uptown and ask some questions. Do you need a ride? I'm sure we can drop you somewhere."

Cecil looked in the back seat again. Peaches hadn't budged and didn't look like he was going to anytime soon. At least not without a large amount of sausage.

"No, thanks," Cecil answered. "I'd hate to keep you from your date with death. I'll call Robert to pick me up. He should be done by now. Please call me if you survive your visit or if anything happens with the car."

"Will do," I said.

"Remember, don't let anyone else try and drive it. I'm serious."

"No one but Monty and me can drive the Dark Goat, got it."

He stepped back as I revved the engine.

"It's not called the…Nevermind. This is such a mistake," I heard him say as I pulled away.

FOURTEEN

"WHERE IS THIS place?" I asked.

"Hybrid is located at 1 East 60th Street."

I jumped on the West Side Highway and sped uptown, weaving around the evening traffic.

"What are we walking into? Why did TK have to make a call? Why did Cecil say it was suicide?"

"This is a private establishment."

"I thought it was a hotel? It's a private hotel?"

Monty nodded as I avoided the yellow hazards known as New York City taxicabs.

"Hybrid has two wings, a large one for normals, consisting usually of the entourage, assistants, and servants of the demigods."

"And the other?"

"The smaller, more secure wing, is for the demigods and the occasional deity who happens to be in town."

"So I can't just walk in and get a room?"

"All reservations go through Pollux. He's been known to turn guests away, normal and demigod alike. His word, like his brother Castor's, is absolute within Hybrid."

"Isn't this Pollux the prick who Dex told us to avoid?"

Monty pinched the bridge of his nose and sighed.

"Pollux is a powerful demigod. Do you think you can refrain from using that title around him?"

"Monty, this is me," I said. "I know what tact is."

"Sometimes, I wonder."

"Doesn't sound so dangerous. Why was Cecil so freaked?"

"Because Hybrid is dangerous to non-demigods. People have been known to go missing inside its walls."

I cut across the city, east on 58th Street to Madison Avenue and made a left on 60th Street. A block later, I stopped in front of what used to be the Metropolitan Club. From the looks of things, the place was designed as an impenetrable fortress. The twelve foot wrought-iron fence covered in runes told me Hybrid served an exclusive and select clientele who valued privacy above all else.

The valet stood in front of the Hybrid and gave me a nod when I stopped. He looked at the SuNaTran emblem and pointed a little farther up the block. I parked the Dark Goat in one of the reserved spots and stepped out. Monty looked down the block and narrowed his eyes. I held open the back door and my hellhound unsprawled, shaking his body once outside.

<Can we go to the place?>

<We need to go in this place and ask questions.>

<About meat? I can answer your questions.>

<No. Not about meat. We're kind of busy right now.>

<You can never be too busy for meat. Meat is life.>

<Meat is not life. Meat is meat. What does that even mean anyway…meat is life? Who taught you that?>

<It is a basic truth. If you understood, you wouldn't be asking that question.>

<We'll get meat later. I swear, how do you eat so much? >

I nudged Peaches over to the side. He moved about two inches before I felt the strain on my knee. Somehow, my hellhound had discovered Zen through the process of devouring ungodly amounts of meat. He'd be asking me the sound of one sausage falling soon.

"Make sure you keep to the designated path, Simon."

"Why?" I asked, holding the handle of the Goat until I heard the anvil locking sound. "Will I get lost in the dark forest?"

"No, you will step into the abundance of oblivion circles around the property, placed there to dissuade intruders from attempting the fence."

<Do you see the circles with symbols on the ground?>

<Yes, they feel bad.>

<Good. I need you to stay away from them.>

<They're good, not bad?>

<No. they're bad, stay away from them.>

<You just said they're good. Are they good or bad?>

<Bad. Stay away from them.>

<Are you hungry? Sometimes when I'm hungry I get confused too. Do you need some meat? Remember that meat is...>

<No. Just stay away from the circles.>

<Sometimes when I'm hungry I get cranky too.>

<I'm not cra—Just stay away from them.>

"Oblivion circles, that would be bad," I said, keeping to the path designated with faintly glowing runes.

"Indeed." Monty adjusted his sleeve and followed the door attendant inside. I opened my jacket and made sure I had access to Grim Whisper and Ebonsoul. "Make sure your creature doesn't step in one as well."

"Taken care of. Do you think they have meat inside?"

"For you or your creature?" Monty said with a slight smile.

"Oh, ha ha. Yes, because I usually go around craving meat. For him, of course."

"This is not a local deli or butcher shop. I doubt they have slabs of meat hanging about waiting for the transient hellhound. Is this going to be a problem?"

"No, let's just do this. I'll keep an eye on him."

The Hybrid had kept the original lobby of the Metropolitan Club when they acquired the property. A grand double staircase led to an arcade on the second level, overlooking the reception area. A large, rust-colored Bokhara Persian rug dominated the center of the floor.

Spaced evenly around the rug were clusters of wingbacks grouped in threes, providing little capsules of privacy for some of the guests. The impressive wood ceiling fit right in with the abundant use of gold-leaf and marble. The only word that fit the building was palatial.

It whispered old money and extravagance and I was sure J.P. Morgan would be proud to see it had been maintained in the same condition as the Metropolitan Club. Opposite the grand staircase, a marble fireplace large enough to burn a small forest held a raging fire.

Places like this usually made me upset. It smacked of elitism and privilege. The people who used these places only did so because they belonged to a certain group. In this case—demigods. It wasn't through any merit on their part. I don't know what pissed me off more, the fact that they acted superior to normals or that normals actually believed they were superior.

After a few recent encounters with gods, my overall impression of deities, full or half, was that power drove them round the bend on a straight road. The ones that appeared sane were actually scarier than the ones that were batshit out of their minds.

I stopped in the center of the reception area and looked around at the old-world opulence, impressed they had kept the building in such good shape. One cluster of wingbacks was occupied by a couple—a young man, and woman. I walked by and overheard a snippet of the conversation.

"And I told him to get with the times," the man said. "Email is a real thing now. Why do I have to keep delivering messages? Do you know what he said?"

"I can imagine," the woman answered. "You know he's set in his ways."

"He goes: 'Hermes, it's your job, it's what you do. You deliver messages. Aren't you faster than this email?"

"He actually asked if you were faster than email?" the woman inquired with a short laugh. "He's never going to embrace technology, you know."

"Don't remind me. I swear it makes me want to go Roman."

I kept walking around reception until Monty coughed and caught my attention. He stood at the front desk speaking to an older woman.

The woman gave me a cursory glance and then focused on Monty again. Her nametag read Erin F. Uries, and she gave me a tight smile when I stepped close to the large desk. Her brown eyes glimmered violet for a moment, and I felt the energy surrounding her.

She glanced down at Peaches and then focused on Monty again.

"Name, please?" She looked down at the monitor in front of her.

"Montague—Tristan Montague."

"Purpose of stay?"

"We're not staying. I'm here to see Castor."

She glanced at Monty again. "Did someone arrange this meeting?"

"TK Tush."

"Thank you." Erin nodded and entered some data into her computer with a quick tapping of keys. "Mr. Castor will be with you shortly. You can wait in the bar or reception." She motioned to the wingbacks.

"I could use a cuppa," Monty said, heading to the bar.

We sat at the bar, and Monty requested a cup of Earl Grey. He was looking a bit worn out, and I wondered if the Reckoning had taken a higher toll than I imagined. What we needed was a vacation. A non-magical, non-monster-trying-to-kill-us vacation.

"For a second I thought you were going to say a martini—shaken, not stirred. What was that with the name?"

He waved my words away and subtly looked

around the room. The bar was on one side of the hotel restaurant. Empty tables filled the floor, but I saw activity in the kitchen area on the far side of the room.

"Simon, you need to stay alert." Monty sipped his tea and grimaced. "They call this tea?"

"I am alert. I mean as—"

"We aren't demigods."

"No kidding, really? What was your first clue? What are you talking about? Of course we aren't demigods."

"This entire establishment was created to cater to demigods and their appetites. If we handle this questioning poorly, we'll have to deal with a hotel full of upset half-deities. Is that a scenario you want to entertain?"

"How many demigods are we talking about?"

"Are you insane?" He stared at me as if I had sprouted another head.

"What? It's purely an academic question. Do we think our Mr. Crazy Eyes is here?"

"There's a good chance. If not, Castor may know how to find him."

"And he would share that information? With us?"

"There's always a cost." Monty nodded and took another sip. "We still need to ask."

"Do you think he will answer?"

"Depends on the question," a voice said from behind us.

FIFTEEN

"HELLO, CASTOR." MONTY sipped more of his tea and turned to face the man behind us. "Your Earl Grey needs considerable work."

"I'll make sure to look into it," Castor said with a raised eyebrow. "I heard about Connor. I'm sorry for your loss."

Castor was dressed in a gray suit and managed to look as if he had just left a photoshoot for the latest men's magazine. I wondered if gods had the equivalent of a divine High Street where they all shopped. If I remembered my mythology correctly, both Castor and Pollux were immortal, after Pollux shared his immortality with his brother.

His gray hair was carefully cut and coiffed. He looked at us with an expression of mild amusement and curiosity. He gave Peaches a wide berth and moved to stand next to Monty.

"Thank you." Monty placed the cup on the bar.

"How is Pollux?"

"You know him, busily up to something as usual. TK said you would be visiting. Is it true you two had a Reckoning?"

Monty gave him a short nod. "Yes."

"Incredible," Castor said and slowly shook his head. "And you're still alive. You are either favored or skilled."

"Favored." Monty pulled out the picture of Crazy Eyes and placed it on the bar next to his tea. "Speaking of favors, do you know who this is?"

Castor leaned in to look at the picture. Recognition flitted across his face, but he quickly masked it. "May I?" He reached to remove it from the bar.

Monty placed a finger on the picture.

"No, I think I'll hold on to this for a moment longer," Monty said, keeping the photo on the counter. Castor withdrew his hand slowly. "Have you seen him?"

Castor started shaking his head. "I don't think —"

"I didn't think it was possible to do a runic capture on a deity." Monty held up the picture and Castor's face darkened. "Even a half-deity should have the ability to mask his presence from a group of humans working for the NYTF with rudimentary equipment. Don't you agree?"

"Not here." Castor looked around the bar. "My office."

He turned and left. Monty took another sip of his tea before following.

"A runic capture?" I looked at the photo still on the counter. "Isn't it just a picture?"

"No. Deities have the ability to mask their images from cameras and other recording devices. You can't get their image unless they allow it."

"What do they do, vibrate their faces really fast?"

"The runic interference coming off of them requires specifically enhanced equipment. This image was taken against this particular person's will. It's probably the reason he killed them."

"How did they get this picture of Crazy Eyes?"

Monty took another sip of his tea. "I don't know. Maybe we should go ask Castor and find out?"

We left the bar and headed up the grand staircase. At the top of the staircase, we turned right down a wide corridor. At the end of the corridor stood a large door that was slightly ajar.

Monty pushed the door and we entered the cavern that was Castor's office. The rooms in the Hybrid were spacious. This one felt large enough to land a plane in. I felt as if we had stepped into the Greek wing of a museum.

Art and sculptures lined the walls. At the far end, a desk made of marble took up one entire side of the room. Three floor-to-ceiling windows along the west wall provided an excellent view of 5th Avenue and Central Park.

I noticed the guards right away and counted six of them spaced out around the office. They stood several inches over my six feet. Dark combat armor covered their massive frames, and each held some kind of bladed weapon in his hands. They remained motionless as we walked by. Even when I stepped close to one, he didn't flinch.

"Why would a demigod need security?" I asked Monty under my breath. "Isn't he immortal? What threat would require security?"

"Maybe a mage, an immortal detective, and his hellhound make him nervous?" Monty replied. "Keep your wits about you. The guards are not human."

"What are they?"

"Something that should be impossible. Remember Hades with Valkyries? This is worse."

"What is worse than Valkyries?" I shuddered at the thought of them.

Monty said nothing more and kept walking.

I glanced over at the nearest guard. I let my senses expand and felt for an energy signature. Nothing.

"Please, come in," Castor said from behind his slab of a desk. "Door."

One of the guards stepped over and secured the door, standing in front of it, effectively blocking our exit. Every surface of the office was covered in runes. Some were blatant, others were subtle and partially hidden. None of them looked friendly.

"Can you cast in here?"

"I don't want to find out. Let's start with diplomacy."

"Every time we start with diplomacy, we end up fighting for our lives."

"I think this time will be different. He seems reasonable. It's his brother who's somewhat deranged."

We were halfway across the hangar of an office when Castor cleared his throat to speak

"I'm afraid I'm going to need you to leave that picture with me, Tristan," Castor said and flashed an apologetic smile. "If you don't comply, I will be forced to detain you."

I crossed my arms and nodded to Monty. "Go on, unleash the diplomacy," I said with a wave of my hand. "Because I'm sure 'detain' is just code for dinner at the restaurant downstairs."

Monty glared at me and kept walking forward. I placed my back to the wall and rested a hand on Grim Whisper, in case the guards got the sudden impulse to de-statuefy and get stabby. Peaches, sensing something was off, started a low-pitch rumble next to me and entered 'advanced shred' mode.

<Be ready, boy. I don't think Monty is going to convince him to be nice.>

<Can I bite them?>
<Only if they move to hurt us.>
<I don't like how they don't smell.>
<They don't smell?>
<No smell. Like the old man at the place.>

"Well, that can't be good," I whispered.

Peaches chuffed and kept growling. The muscles along his flanks rippled with coiled energy. I noticed his runes were dormant and wondered if it was an effect of the symbols all around us.

Monty took a few more steps forward and held out the picture. Castor nodded and motioned to one of the guards. The guard stepped over quietly and removed the photo from Monty's fingers. He glided over and placed it on Castor's desk.

"That was a wise choice." Castor sat behind his desk. "Your response will dictate my next course of action. I advise honesty."

Monty pulled on one sleeve and brushed some hair from his face. He narrowed his eyes at Castor.

"Ask."

"Do you know who this is?" Castor held up the picture. "Do you know his name?"

"'Crazy Eyes'?" I volunteered.

"No," Monty said, ignoring me. "If I had that information, there would be no need for my presence here. I take it *you* know, however."

Castor nodded. "I'm afraid I can't share that information with you or your partner."

"You don't want to do this," Monty said, his

voice a promise of obliteration. "We could just leave. Allow us safe passage out of the Hybrid."

"I can't. Pollux left explicit instructions. It's too risky to let you leave." Castor looked at the guards. "Kill them."

SIXTEEN

THE GUARDS STEPPED away from the walls, hefting and swinging their weapons as they approached us.

"I don't think anyone shares your definition of diplomacy," I said, drawing Grim Whisper. "What are they?"

"Einherjar."

"As in fallen warriors Odin is keeping around to deal with the end of the world?"

"They will fight beside him against the giants, at least according to the myth."

"How did they end up here? I thought they were off in Valhalla, feasting and training for Ragnarok?"

"They're supposed to be, but things aren't always as they should be." A soft wail escaped the blades as Monty pulled out the Sorrows. "Maybe we should ask Castor?"

"I'm guessing no casting?" I drew Ebonsoul with my other hand. "Casting would be really useful right about now. Maybe an anti-Einherjar area spell? That would be fantastic."

"The runes in here dampen any casting." He gave me a quick look. "Coming here was not the best of ideas."

"Your powers of understatement almost leave me speechless." I gave him a sidelong glance. "Are they immortal?"

"Undead. There's a difference. Your gun will be useless. Negation rounds can't negate something that's been negated."

"What?"

"Use your blade." He pointed to Ebonsoul. "That should work."

"Couldn't you just say that without trying to give me a brain cramp? Would speaking clearly kill you?"

"I always speak clearly. You never pay attention."

I holstered Grim Whisper and saw Castor lean back in his seat with a smile. I made a mental note to slap that smile off his face if we survived this. I looked down at my always ready-to-pounce hellhound.

<You see the man sitting at the desk over there?>

<That one smells bad. Yes.>

<You can go bite him…a lot. Make sure he doesn't get away. >

Peaches winked out and reappeared next to a

surprised Castor. To his credit, Castor recovered quickly and jumped back out of his seat, avoiding a large arm-removing chomp. Peaches shredded the armrest and spit it out next to the desk.

My attention was diverted by the whistling sound of agony headed my way. I pressed the main bead on my mala bracelet, forming a shield in time to deflect a battle-axe intent on bisecting my head.

The weapon bounced off the shield and fell to the ground. The next second it flew back across the office and into the hand of the Einherjar who'd thrown it.

"No fair," I said from behind my shield. "Automatic weapon-retrieval is against the rules."

"There's only one rule," Monty said, sliding forward and impaling one of the Einherjar while ducking under the slash of a broadsword. He whirled around and removed the head of another Einherjar who went still and became dust a second later. "Don't lose your head."

"I swear, if you say there can be only one…" I backpedaled from a vertical slash and skipped out of reach from a lunge. "I'll stab you myself."

Another Einherjar closed on me. Their silent attacks were eerie. This one slashed at my leg. I lowered my shield and stepped into his attack. He reversed direction and slashed upward. I saw the feint too late. My guard was open, exposing my neck.

A loud wail filled my ears as Monty's sword

blocked the Einherjar's blade from cutting into my neck. Monty kicked forward, forcing my attacker to bend forward. I slashed down and removed his head. He burst into dust before hitting the floor. There was no siphon from Ebonsoul. The Einherjar held no energy signature.

"I said keep your head, not lose it." Monty slid to the side and parried a thrust aimed for his midsection. "Remember, in the end there can be none."

I swear I saw a smile cross his lips. The Sorrows gave off a blue glow as he quick-stepped forward, fencing style, and buried one of his swords in the chest of an approaching Einherjar. He gestured and the sword's wails became a scream. The Einherjar burst into a cloud of dust. My shield dropped a few seconds later.

"I thought you couldn't cast?"

I heard the growling and stole a glance behind me. Peaches had latched on to Castor, who was putting up a fight by attempting to pummel my hellhound. I wasn't worried, though. Peaches' head had been smashed through brick walls. It was only slightly thicker than my own.

"I'm channeling the energy through my weapons, which magnify the effect." He shoved me back just as another battle-axe sailed past us, burying itself in the wall behind us. "Look out."

I looked as the axe began to wiggle out of the wall in an effort to return to its owner.

"Oh, hell no," I growled, running at the unarmed, undead, axe-thrower. I drew Grim Whisper and fired as I closed on him. He bared his teeth as the rounds punched into him, doing nothing. He outstretched one arm to the side and grinned.

I heard the axe come loose from the wall.

"Simon, the axe!" Monty yelled.

I slid forward, reached the Einherjar, and grabbed his outstretched trunk of an arm. I twisted it behind him with an added shove forward. The Einherjar looked at me, surprised for all of two seconds, as he stumbled into the axe's trajectory, giving himself the ultimate haircut from the neck up. He dissolved into dust a second later.

The remaining two Einherjar flanked Monty. I fired Grim Whisper to distract one and had to jump to the side to avoid a flying hellhound. Peaches hit a column, slid across the floor, and stood growling. He shook off the blow and rumbled at Castor. It took me a few seconds to register that his collar was glowing bright red before he blinked out. He blinked in again a second later, twice his normal size.

<Bondmate, I have increased my mass. Please step out of my path.>

"Monty, move!" I pushed him against the wall as Massive Peaches barreled through the Einherjar, shredding the remaining two with several quick snaps of his jaw on his way to mangle Castor.

"That may be problematic," Monty said, sheathing his swords. "We need Castor alive. Can you stop your creature?"

I ran after Peaches.

<Boy, don't kill him. We need him alive.>

Peaches stopped mid-stalk and turned his head to face me. His eyes held a faint red glow and the runes along his body were increasing in intensity. He was a few seconds away from his eye-beam maneuver.

<He has attacked me physically and poses a potential threat to you and the angry mage. Logic dictates I remove this threat. Can I masticate on his leg?>

<Logic? When did you become Vulcan? No. No masticating.>

<I am not Vulcan. I am a hellhound, offspring of Cerberus, my sire. Are you well, bondmate? Have you received a head injury?>

<I'm fine. Don't blast him, yet. Let Monty ask him some questions first. If he tries to attack, then unleash your omega beams.>

<If by omega beams, you mean my baleful glare, then I will restrain myself from their use for the time being.>

<Thanks. Can you go back to a less massive size?>

<After the questioning, and if the target no longer poses a threat.>

Castor was a wreck. His neatly pressed suit was missing both sleeves and his jacket was torn in several other places. His hair, which had been model-shoot ready when we'd met, was now a disheveled disaster. He had cuts and scratches all over his face and arms. One of his pants legs was missing a large Peaches-chomp-sized section.

The three of us approached a shaken Castor. He kept the desk between us and reached into a drawer for something. Peaches nudged the desk and shoved Castor back into his chair.

I almost felt sorry for him, until I remembered he'd unleashed the Einherjar on us.

"Keep that hellhound away from me!" Castor pointed. "Do you know how expensive this suit was?"

"Who is Crazy Eyes, the man in the picture?" I pointed to the photo on the desk. "Tell me who he is."

"He checked out several days ago. This is all Pollux's doing. I told him to refuse the reservation."

"What is his name?" Monty stepped closer to the desk and took the picture. "His *real* name."

"I don't know. I heard Pollux call him Sal."

"Is he a demigod?" I asked. "Who is the god part of this equation?"

"I don't know." Peaches growled. "Wait!" Castor looked at me. "He's a demigod, a powerful one. More than you'll be able to handle with just your hound."

"Do you know where we can find him?" Monty asked. "It's urgent we speak with him."

"Urgent? You speak with him?" Castor broke

out in laughter. "After today, I wouldn't worry about that too much. I'm certain he'll find you."

"Was he alone? Did this Sal person check out alone?"

"No, he was accompanied by an older gentleman."

"Did this older gentleman have a name?"

"You'd have to ask Pollux, he handled their stay at the Hybrid. Why don't you wait until he returns? I'm sure he'd be happy to assist you."

"No, thanks." I sheathed Ebonsoul and looked over at Monty. "We need to bail."

Monty looked around the destruction in the office and turned back to Castor.

"Where did you get Einherjar?"

"I didn't," Castor snapped back. "That was Pollux, and—before you ask—I don't know how he got them. He just said to eliminate anyone asking for Sal. Where did *you* get a hellhound?"

"I didn't," Monty replied and glanced at me. "*He* did."

"You're bonded to the hellhound? You're a *human*."

"Not until I've had my coffee."

"Where did you get it?" Castor asked with a mixture of surprise and disgust clear in his voice.

"Hades." I noticed movement among the piles of dust. "And his name is Peaches. He's not an 'it.'"

"Hades would never give away one of Cerberus' pups to someone like you." He scoffed. "Did you steal *it?*"

This guy was beginning to piss me off, so I did the one thing all beings with power hated. I ignored him.

"Monty," I said, giving Castor my side but keeping an eye on him, "Is that dust moving?"

"What dust?" Monty turned to see piles of dust reforming into the bodies of the Einherjar. "Spontaneous reintegration. Fascinating."

"No...not fascinating, disturbing. Extremely disturbing."

My eye caught more movement. Castor moved to the side and placed his hand on the desk, causing a panel to glow. Metal shutters slammed down over the windows. A thick steel plate slid down and covered the door. Our only exit.

"The dampening runes in here will prevent any teleportation circles, and the Einherjar will just keep coming back. It's what they do. No matter how many times you kill them, they will come back. Don't you know the story? They're getting ready for the end."

"Remind me to end you when I get a chance," I said, kicking away some of the dust only to see it flow back and continue to solidify.

"You'll never get that chance. I'll have the staff come up and remove what's left of your bodies." He pressed another section of the desk and a rift opened behind him.

"Don't let him get—" I lunged forward. Peaches

reacted faster than I did. He bounded over the
desk and landed where Castor had been a half-
second earlier.

The piles of dust were beginning to resemble
bodies. Monty crouched and picked up some of
the dust. It flowed out of his hand and rejoined
the pile.

"This spell is stronger than anything Pollux or
Castor can cast. Someone or something much
stronger is behind this."

He gestured and white runes floated from his
fingers. A few moments later, they faded and
disappeared. He gestured again, and a teleportation
circle formed and vanished before it was complete.

"Well, he wasn't lying about the dampening
runes."

"No, he wasn't." Monty looked down at the piles
around the office. "I'd say we have about ten
minutes before we're facing reintegrated
Einherjar."

I narrowed my eyes and noticed that the metal
shutters that blocked the windows and door were
covered in runes.

"I'm open to ideas. If you can't cast, there's no
way my orb is making an appearance. May as well
stick a fork in us…we're done."

"That,"—Monty tapped his chin—"is an
excellent idea."

He stepped quickly to the east wall and stood in
between two of the shutters, blocking the

windows. He drew the Sorrows and let energy flow into them. They began giving off a bright blue light.

"What is an excellent idea?" I shielded my eyes from the arc-welding brightness of the Sorrows. The wails from the swords were getting louder.

"I'm going to insert the Sorrows into this section of the wall and set off a sonic resonance wave."

"That wall is marble." I looked around the office. "All the walls are marble."

"Everything has a frequency, even marble. The Sorrows will act like a fork—a tuning fork. The wave will weaken the marble and then perhaps"— he looked back at Massive Peaches—"your creature can lend us his bark."

"You want Peaches to run into a marble wall?"

"Not into—through." Monty looked at the reforming Einherjar. "Unless you have an alternative, I'm open to ideas."

<The theory is sound, bondmate, provided the stone has been compromised. I can lead with a bark and my baleful glare.>

<How loud? Like Tate Modern loud?>

<Louder.>

"This bark he's planning to use is louder than what he did at the Tate. I'm not sure that's such a good—"

"Simon, we're running out of time."

"Fine. If he demolishes the building, it's your

fault."

"He's *your* hellhound." Monty looked at Peaches. "Can he do it?"

I crouched down and rubbed Peaches' flanks.

<You can get hurt. I don't want you getting hurt.>

<I understand your concern, but I am a hellhound. I can sustain considerable amounts of impact without taking damage. I can do it.>

"Peaches agrees. As long as the stone is weak, he thinks he can break through." I looked down at my hellhound and rubbed his head. "Monty, make sure that wave works."

Monty nodded and stepped to the wall. "On my signal, make sure he runs in *between* the swords." Monty lunged forward and buried the Sorrows in the marble easily. Still holding them, he whispered something under his breath and took several steps back.

<In between the swords, or you won't go through.>

<Understood.>

The piles of Einherjar dust were almost reformed. The wails of the Sorrows increased in pitch and volume. I saw Peaches' eyes glow red as cracks formed in the marble. He fired his omega beams, knocking off a chunk of the marble wall. He pushed off with his hind legs, cracking the floor, and bounded at the wall head-first.

SEVENTEEN

OUT OF THE corner of my eye, I saw the first Einherjar stand. He extended an arm and caught a battle-axe. Peaches ran at the wall, unleashing a bark that brought me to my knees. The shockwave from the bark smashed the Einherjar into a wall, reverting it to dust again.

I pressed the main bead on my mala bracelet, formed my shield, and crouched down. Monty slid in next to me while jagged marble shrapnel pounded my arm and flew past us. Peaches smashed into and through the wall, landing outside with a crash.

I felt the tremors run through the floor as some of the other Einherjar began to stand. The sound of shattering glass filled the office.

"There's a good chance your creature just compromised the integrity of a load-bearing wall." Monty removed the Sorrows from the wall and sheathed them.

"How do you know it's load-bearing?" I said, stepping up to our new exit and looking down at 5th Avenue below. "Could just be aftershocks from the initial impact."

Monty pointed to the other side of the office, and I saw the floor sway. "It may be time to bail?"

I nodded and stepped through the gaping hole in the wall. It could easily fit a small SUV into the space and still have room on either side.

"This building is old." I looked at the outside of the Hybrid. "Maybe it was due a renovation?"

"Not like your creature has given them a choice."

Monty leaped off the parapet wall that encircled the second floor. He landed silently and looked up at me before walking to the Dark Goat. Peaches, back to normal size, sat on his haunches and waited for me to come down.

All around the Hybrid, I heard alarms going off. The metal shutters tried to rise, but the frames were skewed and no longer square, causing them to get stuck in their tracks. Red strobe lights shone into the night all around the property. I peeked back into Castor's office and saw two more of the Einherjar had reformed.

"Time to bail," I said and jumped off the ledge of the second story. I landed next to Peaches, who padded next to me as we walked rapidly to the

Dark Goat.

<Can you have the angry man make me some meat?>

<After that, you deserve it. But you know, Monty doesn't eat meat. Why don't we go to the place and get you some extra meat?>

<Meat is life…extra meat is…>

Peaches stopped and howled into the night.

<My thoughts exactly.>

I opened the back door, and Peaches bounded in, rocking the Dark Goat. I turned back to see Castor stepping quickly out of the Hybrid with a group of men in combat armor. None of them were Einherjar. He had a phone to his ear and stared sharp poison-tipped daggers at me. I waved as I jumped into the Dark Goat and pulled away.

I heard a deep rumble and looked into the rear-view mirror to see more of the Hybrid collapse and fall into the street. I headed downtown on 5th Avenue to get my amazing hellhound his pastrami special.

"Can you call him?" Monty adjusted his seatbelt.

"Why aren't we being chased by Einherjar right now?"

"Whoever summoned them interlaced a containment component to the spell. They must stay within the walls of the Hybrid. If they were to step outside of the property they would most likely return to Valhalla."

"That sounds like it takes some serious power." I

swerved around some yellow moving deathtraps otherwise known as NYC taxicabs. "Who could do that? Wait, call who?"

"George Rott. Call him."

"I don't have a number for him." Then I remembered his last call. Even though the number was unknown and blocked, I had a way. "I know someone who might, though."

I dialed the only one who could help. The Hack.

The call took a few moments as it bounced across several sites and then piggybacked on another line in a backhaul. From there, it jumped to a T3 line and rerouted the call, repeating the process several times. Hack had tried to explain it to me one time. All I got was that it made it impossible to trace the call.

He picked up after a long silence.

"Simon, Simon, you're back. You were dark, and now you're not. You were cold, and now you're hot. So hot...too hot. They're looking for you, the hot ones."

"Hello, Hack." I knew better than to try to understand any of what he said. Some days his hackspeech was clear and almost lucid, other days it just sounded like random words strung together. I needed to get right to the point. The Hack never stayed on the phone long. "I need a number and an address, if you can back-trace it from a call."

"Date and time? We're all running out of time, Simon. It's getting so hot...so hot."

I gave him the date and time of George's call.

"Let me digest this. I'll send you the information. Hack out!"

I hung up and pocketed the phone.

"How is your friend doing these days? He still sounds quite deranged. Is he getting enough oxygen on the planet he inhabits?"

"Hack is one of the most dangerous cybercriminals I've ever encountered. Every three-letter agency on the planet fears, admires, and wants to capture him. He may be a little off, but his info is always solid."

"A little off? Your Hack is *beyond* a little off."

"He kept mentioning being hot. Do you think it has something to do with dragons?"

Monty rubbed his chin. "I would imagine even someone who exists in a dimension of his own making could be aware of the shifts in power, even if he's off—or perhaps because he's off."

"We're all a little off. Hack just doesn't like going outside, or people, or conversations lasting longer than twenty seconds. Okay, he may be more than a *little* off."

Monty nodded and looked out the window.

"How much heat are we looking at for the redecoration of the Hybrid?"

"Pollux will be livid. The Hybrid is sacred to him, and we just destroyed a large section of it. I'm sure that whatever he's planning with this Sal individual has just become personal for us."

"Wonderful, I've always wanted pissed-off demigods after me."

"I'd say you've acquired quite an assortment of angry beings who would like to see you eliminated. Well done."

"Was that supposed to be encouragement? Maybe you should take up demotivational speaking?"

"Are we headed to Ezra's?"

I nodded and pointed behind me with a thumb. "Figured he earned his meal this time. We have some time before Hack calls back."

I looked in the rear-view mirror at the semi-dozing monstrosity taking up all of the backseat.

"He did earn this meal." Monty glanced back. "I'm curious why his runes weren't dampened in Castor's office. He was still able to go interstitial and increase his mass."

"Well, he's not a mage. It's possible his abilities have a different source."

Monty stared at me as I parked in front of Ezra's Deli. "That's not entirely a bad theory. It could be the runes on his body derive their power from an older, more obscure pool of power."

"Or, and this is just my theory, it could be that all that magic meat he eats imbues him with latent sausage magic that refuses to be dampened."

"Sausage magic?" Monty shook his head and got out. "I should've known it was too coherent to be true."

"Are you going to eat? You know Ezra is going to say you've lost weight."

"He's worse than Nana. I could use a cuppa. Whatever they were trying to pass off as tea at the Hybrid was a monumental failure."

Peaches unsprawled as I opened the back door and headed for the deli before either of us. He sat in front of the door, patiently vibrating with delight and anticipation.

<The place where meat is life. Can we go in now?>

<Let me lock the car. Then we can ask if Ezra has some of that low-fat pastrami I've been promising you.>

<We discussed this.>

<No, we didn't. You can barely get in the car without giving it a flat tire. You need to lose some weight.>

<Why? The more mass I have, the more effective I am. Pastrami and all related meats are essential for my wellbeing, and the safety of humankind.>

<The heavier you are, the less healthy you are.>

<You have me mistaken for human. I am a hellhound. More is always better with hellhounds and meat.>

I shook my head and closed the door. *<I'm still going to ask for a low-fat option, you black hole.>*

I put my thumb on the door handle and heard the doors lock. The familiar sound of a hammer striking an anvil came from under the hood. An orange and violet glow flashed over the Goat and faded slowly.

"Could be you don't have refined demigod taste buds." I pushed opened the door to the deli. "It's possible you can't physically experience the sublime greyness of the Earl Grey at the Hybrid."

"It wasn't tea. It was swill."

I stepped inside and took a moment to absorb the place. Peaches strode in and made a beeline for the table in the corner where an old man sat alone. At first glance, he appeared to be an old Jewish scholar. The yarmulke he wore was covered in runes that gave off a faint glow.

Ezra was dressed in his usual white shirt with black pants and black vest. He was poring over a thick book and sipping tea. Monty approached the table and pulled out a chair. I hung back to enjoy the bustling energy of the place.

Photos of celebrities covered the walls. Small tables, which sat four, filled most of the floor space. Some of the tables were occupied with patrons either eating or having lively conversations, even at this hour.

Ezra kept the place open twenty-four hours a day. A large wooden counter ran across one wall with men behind it who were serving drinks and food. He looked up from his book and signaled to a waiter, who came over immediately.

"Pastrami and eggs for him"—he pointed at me —"and twenty pounds of pastrami for the puppy, in his special bowl. Also, a cup of our best Earl Grey for his partner. Steeped for four minutes, not a second more."

"Ezra, it's the middle of the night. Pastrami, and

eggs?"

"You're looking thin. How was London?"

"Memorable and enlightening."

"So I heard, shieldbearer." Ezra placed his hands on the table and looked at Monty. "It pained me to escort your father so early. I'm sorry for your loss, he loved you very much, but it was his time. Are you sure you won't have something to eat?"

"Thank you for your sentiment. It's profound coming from you."

Ezra waved Monty's words away.

"No food, then?"

"That cup of your best Earl Grey sounds spot on, thank you."

"Suit yourself, but you could stand to eat some more. We have a vegetarian and vegan menu here." Ezra shrugged. "Mostly leaves, beans, and that white square stuff that isn't meat. What's it called...toe food?"

"Tofu?"

"That's what I said, toe food."

I was about to answer, when a waiter came out with a large titanium bowl full of steaming pastrami and put it on the floor in front of Peaches. He smelled the bowl and proceeded to devour the meat. A few minutes later, my plate arrived, and I followed Peaches' example with a little less abandon. I actually managed to chew my food before inhaling it.

Another waiter came out with a small tray and a

cup of tea with lemons on the side. He placed the tray in front of Monty, who proceeded to inhale the aroma before taking a sip and closing his eyes in gratitude.

"Now, this…this is tea," Monty said with a groan. "How do you do this?"

"Like anything else, practice."

"Really?" I shook my head at Monty. "Do you need some privacy with your tea?"

Ezra glanced over at the black-hole pastrami-vacuum known as Peaches and petted him on the head. No one else ever touched Peaches while he ate. It was a good way to lose an arm or two. Pastrami went a long way with my hellhound.

"Your bond has grown since I last saw you two." Ezra narrowed his eyes at me. "Not the only bond you've been working on I see, good."

"He's done some serious growing, that's for sure. In London he grew to the size of a small bus."

"He'll do that and more. Who did you find to make him a collar of entropy stones?"

"TK Tush from Fordey Boutique."

"Is there another TK out there I don't know about?" Ezra said with a smile and ran his finger along Peaches' collar. "A regulator and temporal enhancer. This is good work. Is it working?"

"We were just wondering about how it's not affected by some spells or dampeners."

Ezra shook his head and patted the top of Peaches' head again. "This collar is a temporary measure." He pointed at me. "Your *bond* is the real collar. You should get him some training and obedience classes."

"Obedience classes for a hellhound?" I said and chuckled. "Who would offer that? You?"

Ezra nodded. "Actually, yes. My classes are not for beginners, but yes I have trained hellhounds, among other creatures in the past. Cerberus is one of mine."

"You're serious?" I said in disbelief. "You trained Cerberus. To do what?"

"Whatever Hades needed him to do. Specifically, guard the gates of the Underworld. Dead souls allowed in, live souls kept out. We never did work past that whole 'honey-cake' weakness."

"Death trained Cerberus." I shook my head. "That would almost be funny if it weren't true."

"As humorous as I find life and, well, death, I'm not the joking sort. Yes, I'm serious."

"You should consider it," Monty said between sips. "Your creature could use some help. I know for a fact his bondmate could."

"We can discuss that another time." Ezra patted Peaches again. "Why are you here?"

"An angry father plans on making dragons pay for the death of his daughter. In the most violent way possible."

I filled him in on George, Cassandra's death, and George's vendetta on all dragons.

"If he attacks dragons, he could trigger some

nasty consequences and his premature death," Ezra said. "Can you speak to him? Reason with him?"

"Reason with him? Not likely," I said quietly. "George isn't really the reasoning type. He's more the wrecking ball in the china shop kind of person."

"You may have a larger issue than your friend." Ezra opened the book he was studying and turned it to face me. "This is hearsay, but there's a rumor this creature has been spotted downtown."

I looked at the image of a handsome man wearing a sharp black suit with a pale blue shirt and a subdued patterned tie. Behind the man stood the silhouette of something larger and menacing.

The man had pupiless gray eyes to match those in the large shadow behind him. His black hair was parted on one side and kept short on the sides.

"Who or what is that?"

"*That* is a Kragzimik."

Monty raised an eyebrow and sipped more tea. "I thought they were all gone. Wiped out centuries ago."

"A Krag what?" I looked down at the book but had never seen anything or anyone resembling the image. "What's this?"

"That's the image of a nightmare. That is a dragon."

EIGHTEEN

"IS THAT HIS name or the species?"

"It has been both. In this case, it's the classification of an entity. It's a dragon, not a person. He may be using this classification as a name, or not."

"How bad are these Kragzimik?" I turned the book and the image shifted with my perspective, keeping it facing me. "I mean, we've dealt with dragons before."

"*A* dragon," Monty said. "Singular."

"Refresh my memory," Ezra said with a motion of his hand. "How did that encounter with 'Slif' go again?"

It didn't surprise me that he knew about Slif. Very little about the knowledge Ezra possessed surprised me anymore. He was one of the personifications of Death. It meant he had access to information unavailable to anyone else.

"Badly. We lost Cassandra and nearly lost Quan," I replied. "And she wasn't even the real Slif, who I hear is a real off-the-charts scary dragon."

"You dealt with a lesser dragon imposter." Ezra stared at me. "Kragzimik are greater dragons. Several orders of magnitude above what you faced. Usually when one of these appeared in a city"—he pointed at the book—"the city was evacuated or razed to the ground. Sometimes both."

"This is New York City," I said. "We can't do either. Are you suggesting that obliterating the city is easier than dealing with this creature?"

He waved a hand palm down and made a rocking motion. "Eh, it's a toss-up. These things are meshugga."

I looked at Monty. "Don't you have a dragon-ending spell we can use? Something that doesn't require destroying the city?"

He looked at me and gave me the 'are you insane?' look. "We tried that—twice." He sipped some more tea. "I'm not unleashing another void vortex in the city."

Ezra shook his head slowly. "Then I guess you're going to have to face the Kragzimik. He'll probably have a group of young drakes with him. Greater dragons rarely travel alone."

"Drakes? Really. How many?"

"Lots. Have you tested how immortal you are? If you die, are you mostly dead? Being mostly dead is still slightly alive, you know."

"I did die and come back in London. Far as I can tell, I'm mostly immortal," I replied after a brief pause. "Those are the only options, really? Razing, evacuation, or suicide?"

"Well, for an immortal, like you, it's not too bad. You may need to die a few hundred times, but I'm sure he'll get tired eventually. That's when you strike—when he's worn out. Well, after you deal with the drakes. You two—excuse me, three—have chutzpah, I think you can do it."

I stared at Ezra in disbelief. I was conscious of the fact that, whatever my response, this was still Death, with a capital D, whom I was talking to, not an old Jewish scholar. I opted for tact and self-preservation.

"You've really been working on that sense of humor," I said. "I can tell."

"Why would a Kragzimik be active now?" Monty peered over into the book. "Dragons of that age and power rarely get involved in human affairs. They view any living thing that isn't a dragon as insignificant and they measure time in eons."

"The real question is: How do we deal with a Kragzimik? Last time we dealt with a dragon we got our asses kicked, and I distinctly remember being dragonploded."

"How do you deal with any being stronger than you are who's also older, wiser, and able to wield enough power to wipe you off the face of the earth with little effort?"

"Have you and Monty been taking the same demotivational courses?" I asked. "My first answer would be, run away...at speed."

"You find another being just as strong or stronger," Monty said quietly. "And get them to fight each other."

Ezra rubbed the side of his nose with his index finger and pointed at Monty. "Exactly. If a Kragzimik is wandering the streets of this city, he wants something. Something powerful. Find out what that is and convince something stronger to get it."

"Is a demigod as strong as a dragon?" My phone vibrated in my pocket, followed by the Imperial Death March. "I need to take this."

Ezra waved me on as I stood and moved to the corner while he kept speaking to Monty.

Usually it was the one ringtone I dreaded hearing. The Hack used it after he managed to override the settings of my phone. Now it only played when he called. Tonight, this call signified a meeting with George. I took a deep breath, let it out, and connected the call.

"Hello, Hack." I tried to keep my voice light. "What do you have for me?"

"I wanted to send it....send it," Hack said, more agitated than usual. "Too dangerous. Rottweiler chomp! Too dangerous!"

"Slow down, Hack." I kept my voice even and

modulated. "Do you have a number for me?"

Hack read off a string of digits, which I committed to memory. I heard him take a deep breath and exhale.

"This is dangerous, Simon." His voice was calmer and had switched gears into semi-lucid territory. "He was hard to trace. They're good. I'm better. Whatever he's using, it smells military. This George is rotten. Did you see what I did there? Anyway, you should stay away. He's a shadow… black…hidden. Keep away. Verboten!"

I interrupted before Hack entered full-blown ranting territory. "Did you get a location?"

"No. The line is being blocked, or he's keeping it off. My guess is that he's using masking software or something with a geosync to stay in the dark. Be careful with this person. People who need to keep to the shadows are the real monsters. Hack out!"

He hung up.

Monty gave me a glance and a raised eyebrow, which meant: had I gotten anything valuable from my marginally sane cybercriminal contact? I'd become pretty fluent in the language of Montyglance.

I nodded and dialed the number Hack had given me for George. It did the same delay thing, and I imagined it was bouncing and piggybacking all over the place in an effort not to be traced. After a long silence, the call connected.

"Strong." George's voice was a harsh rasp full of

menace and pain. "Took you long enough."

"We need to talk. Face to face."

"Where?"

"Schurz. 0600."

"You bringing the mage?"

"And my hellhound." I paused. "That going to be a problem?"

"No problem. I'll bring my friends, then. Let's take a stroll with John Finley and have one last conversation."

"I'll meet you there."

"Schurz. 0600. Don't be late."

NINETEEN

"DO YOU TRUST him?" Monty asked as we sped uptown.

"Not anymore," I said and stepped on the gas pedal. "In the Company, he was insane, but he defended us. I think *that* George is gone now."

"I didn't get to finish my tea." Monty rifled through the glove compartment. "That's really unacceptable."

"That's your main concern, right now? A cup of tea?"

Monty shot me a glare. "It wasn't *just* a cup of tea. It was near perfection. Perfectly steeped, the water at the right temperature. Exquisite. At least Ezra gave me this."

He held up a small pouch that contained leaves.

"You brought tea leaves with you?"

"*You* carry a flask. Do I criticize your obsession with bean juice?"

"Bean juice? Coffee is ambrosia. Are you kidding me right now?"

"I never kid about tea. Never. All I need now is a cup."

"You...you have a problem."

We had half an hour to get to the park. Carl Schurz Park was a parcel of land that ran from E 84th Street and ended at E 90th Street. It was sandwiched between East End Avenue and the FDR.

Back in my Shadow Company days, urban exercises would be conducted on the grounds. We'd use Gracie Mansion as our base and run ops out of the mayor's home, stretching into the late hours of the night.

Afterward, I would sit on the Esplanade benches, look out over the East River, or walk down to the far end of the park using the small footpath. It was named after John Finley, who was known for strolling around the perimeter of the island.

If I knew George, he'd want to meet at the 86th Street entrance on the Esplanade. It was a perfect trap.

"What are the odds he'll listen to reason and stop this vendetta?" Monty glanced at me, replacing the tea pouch in a pocket. "You trained with him."

"Trained. Past tense. What I remember is what

earned him his nickname. George was a man of singular focus. When he made up his mind to do something, nothing stopped him."

"I don't suppose he'll stop this path of vengeance, considering he lost his daughter to dragons."

"No, not likely," I said, my voice grim. "He'll expect me to take him down. A face-to-face 'talk' only ends with one of us walking away."

"Can you?" Monty asked. "You said you owed him. What will you do when the time comes to stop him?"

"I don't know."

"That's reassuring."

I made a right on 86th Street and headed east into the rising sun.

TWENTY

I PARKED THE Dark Goat in front of the 86th Street entrance. I checked Grim Whisper and tightened Ebonsoul's sheath. I felt Monty looking at me and I gave him a quick, short nod before getting out of the car.

"Let's do this."

I opened the back door, and Peaches rolled out slowly.

<*Did you eat too much?*>

<*I don't understand the question.*>

<*You ate twenty pounds of pastrami. Do you know how much that is?*>

<*I do. Not enough.*>

<*Do you smell any bad men?*>

<*Two. One is very dangerous and smells wrong. The other smells angry and sad, all mixed up.*>

"Two hostiles?" I locked the Dark Goat and headed into the Park. Monty gestured and joined me a few seconds later. "I expected an assault force or at least a hand. If I were George, I'd have this place crawling with my men and then let us come in."

"A classic pincer move." Monty looked around. "Let the enemy approach and then crush them from both sides with overwhelming force."

I nodded. "That's what I'd do."

<*Wait.*> Peaches sniffed the air and turned in a circle. <*All around us, but the smell stays and goes.*>

<*Are you sure the twenty pounds of meat you just ate hasn't short circuited your nose?*>

<*Who said I smelled them with my nose?*>

<*Good point. What does the smell that comes and goes smell like?*>

<*Bad things. Not people.*>

Monty must've seen the look on my face. "What is it?" he asked as I opened my jacket, making sure I had access to my weapons.

"Peaches says two main hostiles, I'm guessing George and his 'friend.' Several more porting in and out all around us." I peered into the park. "I'm not seeing or sensing anything. You?"

"Are you sure your creature isn't delirious from the obscene amount of meat he just ingested?"

"That was my first question. He says they aren't human."

"That can mean one of two things: either Mr. Rott really came here just to talk, but wanted insurance" —it was my turn to give Monty the 'are you insane?' look—"or his friend isn't alone, and he did bring an assault force."

"I'll go with, 'Did he bring an inhuman assault force?' for four hundred, Alex," I said, looking around the park. "Are you sensing anything runic? Oblivion circles or pulverizing traps?"

"Pulverizing traps? When have we *ever* encountered a pulverizing trap?"

"You know, traps that can crush, mangle, or dismember us with extreme pain?"

"You have a hellhound for that."

"We're dealing with demigods. You never know."

He sighed. "Pulverizing traps, indeed," he muttered under his breath. We stood still while Monty narrowed his eyes and scanned the area. "No oblivion circles or *pulverizing* traps that I can see."

I let out a breath in relief and started walking again. "Good." I patted Peaches on the head. "Maybe he just overate. Twenty pounds is a lot of meat."

"Overate? Is that even possible for your creature? That statement implies he has a limit. Something I've yet to witness."

"Makes two of us."

"We still need to proceed with caution."

"You *just* said we were clear of traps."

"That's not to say they don't exist," Monty added. "Just that I can't detect them presently."

"Really?"

Peaches padded next to me and bumped into my leg, nearly knocking my hip out of its socket. "What is it?"

Peaches growled and rumbled. I looked in the direction he was facing. There was motion in the trees, but it was too fast to track accurately.

"I stand corrected," Monty said, looking into the trees and closing his eyes for several seconds before opening them again. "We are presently surrounded by a large amount of beings, though I can't accurately determine what they are."

I looked ahead and saw two figures on the promenade. The sky grew lighter as we approached the circular steps leading up to the Esplanade and a view of the East River.

"Let's not keep them waiting." I gestured forward with my chin and climbed the right staircase leading up. Monty took the left, and we met at the top of the stairs. A broad promenade extended to the right and left. It was deserted, except for the two figures in front of us. One of them leaned casually over the railing and looked into the East River. The other stood, arms akimbo, looking down the stairs and into my face.

A cool breeze whipped off the river and made its way through the park. It was going to be a hot one today, but for now, the warm glow of the sun welcomed us to a new day. I just hoped it wasn't my last.

I recognized George right away. He gazed into

the river with his back to us. I had to look closer to make out akimbo-man. It was Crazy Eyes Sal, who now sported a full beard. Peaches rumbled next to me like a chainsaw on idle. The rumble kicked up a notch when he saw Sal.

<No attacking unless they attack first. I don't know who or what they have around us. Let's be careful.>

<This man smells bad. I will bite him first.>

<Not unless I say so.>

<When you say so, I will bite him first, and often.>

"Hello, Strong," George said, turning to face us. "It's been a while."

"It has. I see you've been keeping busy."

"You could say that." George glanced at Monty. "Make sure your mage keeps his hands where I can see them and no finger movement. We clear?"

"Completely." Monty extended his arms down and to his sides, splaying his fingers. "Will this suffice?"

Crazy Eyes Sal nodded and kept his focus on Monty. I assumed he thought the mage was the greatest threat. I would have agreed before the Sanctuary. Now I'd say I was a close second in the destruction and obliteration department, even though I'd never admit it to Monty.

George wore black combat armor, complete with an armored hood designed specifically for Shadow Company. Two thigh holsters held guns to match the double shoulder holsters. Both calves held two sheaths, each containing large blades.

Each arm contained a forearm sheath, and he wore what appeared to be titanium-laced gloves. I narrowed my gaze and saw he was wearing SuperTac armor. It was the armor used by the Company when facing supernatural threats.

The armor was covered in faintly glowing orange runes that shimmered in the growing sunlight. George was going to war and he was bringing all the weapons.

Recognition focused my attention on one of the shoulder holsters. One of the guns stood out. It was a Taurus Tracker Model 627 in .357 Magnum. Cassandra's hand-cannon. He had modified it. Black energy surrounded and wafted up from the hand-cannon. Entropy rounds.

I ignored Crazy Eyes Sal for the moment and approached George. Sal moved to intercept me, but George shook his head. Sal stepped back and focused on Monty again.

"Looks like you're going to war." I pointed at the arsenal George was wearing. "Where's the invasion?"

George looked down at the weapons he wore. His hand rested on the Taurus and he nodded.

"I have a debt to clear." He looked up at me but kept his hand on the gun. "Either of you have children?"

Silence.

Monty and I both knew what it would mean to have families. Any one of our enemies could and would use them against us. It made us vulnerable, and vulnerability was weakness in the eyes of those who would come after them and us. It was a weakness they would exploit.

I shook my head. George looked off to the side.

"Didn't think so. Why are you here, Strong?"

"Can't let you do this," I replied quietly. "You go after this enclave, these dragons, and you'll start something you won't be able to finish."

"Can't *let* me?" He gave me a dry laugh. "You should be joining me. She died on your watch, Strong. Where the hell were you when a dragon ripped her from me?"

"She knew the danger. I tried to keep her safe, away from the threat."

"You failed."

"What were you thinking?" I pointed at his chest as the anger rose in me. "You think because she was George Rott's daughter she somehow was going to be impervious to danger? She wasn't ready."

"I was thinking that after saving your ass more times than I can count, that the *least* you could do was watch her back and keep her alive."

"You know the risks. How many men, trained men, did we lose in the Company?"

"Save your breath." He glared at me. It was a look of anger, mixed with pain, and something else…despair. "You're wasting your time. Wasting *my* time."

"Doing this won't bring her back."

As soon as I said it, I knew I had made a mistake.

"Save your fucking empty platitudes," he growled and wrapped his hand around the Taurus. "What's next? 'Time will make it easier'? 'I'll get over it'? 'I should choose life'? 'It's not what she would've wanted for me'? 'I need more time to grieve'?"

"Yes, you do. I feel—"

"Shut up, Strong," George rasped, his throaty rumble cutting through my words. "I'll let you in on a little secret. My life is ash. Every day. Every single day is grief. Fuck your feelings. No parent should ever have to bury a child."

"You know she wouldn't want this for you." I let my hand drift over to Grim Whisper. George's eyes had shifted over into 'deadman walking' mode. I'd seen it a few times during my time in the Company. "She wouldn't want you to throw your life away."

Whenever we faced overwhelming odds and there was little chance of walking away, George would shift into this mode. His eyes would go flat, and we knew. He had made peace with death. Over time, the entire squad became known as Rottweiler's Deadmen.

"Life? What life?" George asked, taking a step forward. "You know what I want? I want to wake up in the morning and be able to hug my daughter, but I can't. Do you know why I can't, Strong?"

"George I…" The words escaped me.

"I can't hold my little girl…because a dragon ended her. I'm never going to see her smile again or hear her laugh." His voice dropped to barely above a whisper as he looked out over the river, momentarily lost in a memory. "She had a great laugh, just like her mother."

His face darkened as he turned to look at me again.

"You don't know what you're facing," I said, calmly trying to change the direction of the conversation. "The dragon that kill—took Cassandra from you was nothing compared to what may be waiting downtown. You can't do this alone."

"Who said I was alone?" He glanced over at Crazy Eyes Sal. "Let me introduce you to my associate, Sal."

"I've heard about your demigod friend Sal," I said without looking at Crazy Eyes Sal. I kept my eyes on George because I knew, when it happened, it would start with him.

"Not bad," George said with a nod. "What you may not have discovered at the Hybrid is that Sal is short for Salao."

"He's salty? Sounds like a personal issue. They have creams for that. Have him see a dermatologist."

George smiled, and my stomach clenched. It was a promise of mayhem and death. "You know how

I knew you were scared shitless on missions?"

"My reluctance to run headlong into certain death?"

"You'd try to be funny. I never found you funny, Strong, but here's a fun fact. Something I find genuinely humorous."

We had stepped so far into the twilight zone I half expected to see Rod Serling sitting on a bench.

"Sal here also happens to be the son of a human and Jyeshtha"

Crazy Eyes Sal took a bow with a flourish.

"Oh, bloody hell," Monty said behind me. "Simon, step back."

"Looks like your mage knows," George said with a laugh. "You really should read more."

"Who the hell is Jye—?" I started when I saw the movement and heard Sal speak loudly in a language I didn't understand. I drew Grim Whisper and fired at George. This was going to end now.

A wave of energy blasted me from Sal's direction, and I saw two orbs of flame materialize in Monty's hands.

I was standing two yards away from George. That's when I noticed the pendant similar to my enso around his neck. It gave off a sickly yellow glow as my bullets missed him. For half a second my brain rebelled. How had I missed?

George slid to the side and pulled a forearm blade. I unsheathed Ebonsoul only to have it slip out of my fingers and tumble across the promenade.

"Get away from him, Simon!" Monty yelled as he unleashed his orbs. They flew wide and sailed into the river.

"Monty, what the hell?" I asked, backpedaling. "He's right *there* in front of us." I tripped backward and stumbled. Sal laughed as I landed on my back. I scrambled to my feet as gracefully as a rhino attempting ballet. My coordination was all over the place.

<Get him, boy. Get the bad man.>

Peaches leaped, blinked out, and reappeared at the other end of the promenade. He smashed into the small maintenance hut headfirst, cratering it, and bounced onto the ground, slightly dazed. He shook it off and started stalking.

<No, boy. Stay back. Something is wrong.>

Peaches growled but kept his distance. In the chaos, I had taken my eyes off George. He focused my attention by sliding his blade into my abdomen and grabbing my hair.

I fell to my knees, accompanied by white-hot pain shooting through my body. "It won't be enough," I said through gritted teeth as I held back George's thrust with both hands. My body flushed hot to deal with the damage. "They're stronger than the both of you."

"I know," George said, leaning forward and pressing on the blade with his body weight. "I have an equalizer."

"It doesn't matter what you have," I said with a groan. "Monty, fry this bastard."

"I can't," Monty said, extinguishing the orbs of flame in his hands. "It's too dangerous."

"Dangerous? Burn him!"

Salao laughed again. "You'd be wise to listen to him, human."

"Simon, I might hit *you*."

"You what, ahh!" George twisted the blade. "That's not…really helping."

"Focus, Strong." George slapped me across the face. "I've done my homework. I know this won't kill you, at least not right away."

"Then you know I'm coming for you."

"No. You aren't. I'm going to finish what they started."

"Even if it costs you everything?"

He punched me in the face and drove the blade in deeper. "You're still not *focusing*. Once they stole Cass from me, they took it *all*. I have *nothing* left and nothing left to lose."

"Not…true." I felt the world swim away and come back into focus with sudden pain. "Fuck… you."

"Stay with me, Strong. I don't think we're going to have another conversation after today."

<He's hurting you. Can I bite him?>

<No, boy. Something around him won't let you do it. Stay back, you'll get hurt.>

"You can do this, there's a…there's a

Kragzimik out there. Trust me, you're no match for
—"

"Fairy tales!" yelled Sal. "Kragzimiks are extinct.
Have been for centuries. Stop listening to this...
this *human*. We need to go. Let my men finish
them."

George removed the blade with a sideways
motion reminiscent of seppuku. I looked up into
his eyes, and I knew. He never intended to walk
away from this. They were the eyes of a man who
wanted to see the world burn and was willing to
burn with it.

"They'll know my pain, my daily agony." George
grabbed my hair, pulled my head back, and locked
eyes with me. "I'm going to bring death to their
lives. I'm going to kill everything that's important
to them. Then, at the end—I'm going to erase
them."

He lifted me to my feet, looked down, and saw
my curse had healed the wound.

"I told you," I said with a gasp. "I'll be coming
for you. Both of you."

"You may be healed, but you're not in fighting
condition." George nodded to Sal. "We're done
here. Let's go."

Sal gestured and opened a rift. "This is your last
day, gentlemen. I promise my men will make your
end swift."

"Don't do me any favors, really."

George shoved me back, and I tumbled down

the stairs. By the time I stopped rolling, they were gone.

TWENTY-ONE

MONTY STOOD NEXT to me and drew the Sorrows. Peaches stood over me and growled. My body felt like a furnace from dealing with my injuries. I wiped the sweat pouring into my eyes.

"How many?" I stood unsteadily, using my hellhound for support. "I need to get Ebonsoul."

"And do what? Shave?" Monty gestured, and Ebonsoul appeared at my feet. "He's right. You're in no condition to fight."

"How did I miss him at point-blank range? I never miss." I sheathed Ebonsoul. "How did *you* miss?"

He sheathed the Sorrows and raised a finger. "Shhh, let me focus."

"Go ahead, focus away while we get shredded by Sal's 'men' that aren't really men."

"Can you walk?" Monty scanned the area around us and formed two orbs of flame. "We need to move."

"You want to take a stroll on John Finley Walk?"

"The mansion. It has wards, and we can hold off the impending attack there. If we remain here, we will be overrun. It's not far from here."

"Overrun? That sounds bad."

"Because it is. Let's move."

<That bad man hurt you. Next time I'm going to bite and shake him until his arms and legs fall off.>

The imagery made me laugh, and the pain shut it down immediately. I had to stop to catch a breath.

<Don't make me laugh. When you see him again, you can't go near him until I tell you.>

"Whew, I'm feeling old. No offense."

"None taken, I'm still young by mage standards. Pick up the pace. They're coming."

"I'm moving as fast as I can, I just got seppukued, you know," I snapped. "The next time someone tries to cut you in half, I'd like to see how fast you run afterwards."

"I'm aware of your wound." He turned and unleashed several orbs into the trees behind us. Howls of pain filled the park. "Would you like to explain your difficulties to Sal's minions? I'm sure they would lend you a sympathetic ear, as they reopen the wound and leave your bloody carcass in the park."

"First off," I said, raising a finger and increasing my pace because the howls *were* getting closer, "I wouldn't be a bloody carcass. Second, that was a little dark, even for you."

"It's the middle of the morning, and this park is empty. That doesn't seem odd to you?"

He was right. The Esplanade was usually full of early morning joggers by now.

"Could they have sealed the park?"

"It's likely," he said, gesturing again. "And filled the grounds with dampening runes. The mansion is the only place that feels free of these runes."

"Monty, what exactly is coming after us? I'm just curious since we seem to be running for our lives."

"I think they're drakes." He looked at my wound. "Are you fully healed yet?"

"I know the curse is working, because my body's on fire. I wonder if this is what a menopausal hot flash feels like?" I wiped the sweat from my face. "It's like I took a bath in lava."

"I could always hit you with an orb if you want the full experience."

"Pass," I said, limping faster. "It's taking a little longer than usual to get back up to speed though. Wait, what do you mean you *think* they're drakes? What are drakes doing with Salao?"

"Yes, I think," Monty snapped. "Would you like me to stop and conduct an in-depth interview?"

"No thank you, let's get inside."

We made our way through some trees and came up on the rear of the mansion.

"If these are Sal's 'men,' and I use the term loosely, are we dealing with more of whatever was happening back there?"

"Unlikely. It seems that our mishaps were created by Sal and channeled into that pendant worn by George." He patted his pockets and found the small pouch with tea leaves. "Perhaps there's a cup I can use inside the mansion?"

He pocketed the pouch of leaves and I wondered if Sal had done something to him that I'd missed.

"You need a cup? For your tea? Sure, maybe you can find a cup inside the mansion and finish your tea. It's not like I'm dealing with an evisceration or anything. Don't mind me."

"I'm trying my best not to." Monty pointed to a door at the rear of the mansion. "There. We can get in through there."

I tried the door. "Locked. Do you want to…you know…?" I wiggled my fingers. "Blast it open?"

"No." He shook his head. "I'm still feeling the effects of whatever Sal unleashed on us. How about your creature?"

"He doesn't have opposable thumbs, so how do you want him to open the door?"

"He doesn't have opposable thumbs, but he has an incredibly dense skull, like someone else I know."

"Oh, hilarious." I winced and hunched over as I moved near the mansion. "Go ahead, make fun of the injured."

"If you're still injured, I'll drink a cup of coffee,

black."

I tried to imagine the danger a caffeinated Monty would pose to the Tri-state area and shuddered at the thought.

"Fine." I straightened up. "Don't even kid about you and caffeine."

Monty looked at Peaches. "Have him tap the door without teleporting. Remind him we'd like to stay inside the mansion, not stand in its rubble. He needs to use as little force as possible, but still get past the wards without destroying everything."

I cocked my head to one side and stared at Monty in disbelief.

"Really? *You're* giving advice on how *not* to obliterate a structure?"

"Tell him," Monty said, facing into the park with more orbs in his hands. "Sooner rather than later would be preferable."

<Boy, I need you to open the door. Just nudge it a bit with your head.>

<Do you want me to bark? Like last time?>

<I think Monty wants to keep the house standing. Why don't we hold off on the bark for those things coming after us?>

<Will you make me some meat afterwards?>

<I won't, but Monty will, if you ask nicely.>

<I will. I won't chew his leg or anything.>

<Sounds good. Nudge away.>

Peaches stepped to the door and dropped his head so it bumped against the door. The wards on the doorframe exploded with orange light. The door itself flew into the mansion and smashed against a wall.

We stepped in, and Monty stopped at the threshold. "Let's reinforce the integrity of these wards, shall we?" He gestured, and the door flew back into place. Another motion of his hand and a lattice of orange light filled the doorway, reinforcing it. "That should secure that one."

"You owe him sausage," I said, stepping farther into Gracie Mansion. "And me, an explanation. You could start with how I missed George at point-blank range."

"One second." He gestured again, and an orange sphere erupted from the center of the floor. It grew until it enclosed the mansion. "That will give us some time to formulate a plan."

"What was that?" I looked out the window. Everything was orange tinted through the sphere of energy. "When did you learn that?"

"Something LD taught me."

"How strong is that force field?"

"One moment." Monty raised a finger and headed to the kitchen as a fireball slammed into the sphere, protecting the mansion. It raced across the surface for a few feet before dissipating. The smell of sulphur reached my nostrils. Peaches shook his head at the odor. Monty found a kettle and began boiling water. "This will do."

Monty gestured again and formed two

enormous bratwurst, much to Peaches' delight.
They floated over to a corner, with a salivating
hellhound in hot pursuit. When they fell to the
floor Peaches pounced, sending micro tremors
through the floor.

Monty pulled out his pouch of leaves and
rummaged through the kitchen cabinets for a cup.

"What are you doing?" I asked, staring at him.
"We have incoming. A *mob* of incoming from the
sounds of it. I don't think they're here for high
tea."

"Too early for high tea," he said, mostly to
himself. "What I need are biscuits."

"Biscuits? Tell me that's code for a drake-melting
spell. You know, like a Fiery Biscuit of
Destruction."

"Biscuits. To eat," he said, moving a strand of
hair from his face. "I need some time to process.
Some of these castings are working. Others feel
tenuous."

"We have drakes coming in, Monty." I drew
Grim Whisper and checked the magazine. "Angry
dragon-type beings? Ring a bell?"

"You'll be fine." He opened the cupboard.
"Now, where would they keep biscuits? I thought
people lived here?"

I looked at him. "Are you planning on inviting
drakes in for tea? Haven't you heard there's no 'I'
in team?"

Monty gave up the search for biscuits, when the

kettle signaled the boiling water with a high-pitched squeal. He poured the water into a cup and closed his eyes as the smell of Earl Grey filled the kitchen. He held the cup in his hand and inhaled more of the aroma.

"True, but I'm sure you're aware that there's a 'T,' 'E,' and 'A' in team?" he asked, looking at me. "Now, allow me to focus."

TWENTY-TWO

"WHAT COULD YOU possibly be focusing on that's not drake-related?" I looked out the window again. "Are we not concerned about the creatures coming to share the pain?"

"The sphere should hold them long enough for us to find a way out," he said, peeking through the window. "How did Sal get drakes?"

"I'm more concerned about the 'equalizer' George mentioned. He seemed confident he could take on dragons."

"There was that, as well." Monty rubbed his chin. "Do you think he was bluffing?"

"Does George look like the kind of man who bluffs? If he says he has an equalizer, he has something powerful enough to level the playing field with dragons."

"I don't know of any artifact powerful enough, except perhaps the—" Monty's expression hardened and grew dark. "Oh, bloody hell. We need to get out of here."

"Sal opened a rift. Do you think—?"

Monty gestured and white runes drifted from his hands. They hung in the air for a few seconds before slamming into a window, shattering it.

He shook his head. "This may be a problem. Let me see if I can finish drinking my tea."

"We're going to get barbecued," I said, looking down at Peaches. "At least you can go knowing you had one last cup of your *exquisite* leaf juice."

"Correct, without scalding, burning, or spilling any of my tea. Even the cup is intact. Do you know what this means?"

"You need counseling about your tea drinking?" I looked at him and shook my head." Seriously, Monty, it's just leaves."

"Salao is the son of the goddess Jyeshtha, who is the sister and opposite of the goddess Lakshmi."

"Wait, Lakshmi is the goddess of good fortune."

"Which makes Jyeshtha the goddess of misfortune." Monty held up the cup. "If we were still under the aura of misfortune, it would have been impossible to make a decent cuppa without some calamity occurring. I also noticed the sphere and sausages for your creature were unaffected."

"Aura of misfortune," I said to myself, remembering the pendant around George's neck. "That's how I missed George at point blank."

"And how your creature ended up attacking the

maintenance structure instead of George." Monty nodded. "It appears to be a defensive measure. If you attack George, something goes wrong, like dropping your blade."

"Salao," I groaned. "It also means 'cursed' in Spanish."

"Appropriate, it would seem. We need to get back to Fordey immediately." Monty placed the teacup on the counter. "Their confidence gives me the feeling we may be too late. George didn't say he was *getting* an equalizer."

"No, he said he *had* an equalizer." I still wasn't following. "Why Fordey? The Reckoning is done. LD and TK are gone. I thought they were going to be traveling with Weretigers?"

"Precisely, the boutique will be unattended. It's been a ruse."

"Okay, again. But this time slowly, so I can try and understand what you're saying."

"The equalizer George was talking about. Hekla and her 'security' check. He set us up. He must have been after it for some time. We threw him off when we moved it."

"What exactly was in your tea?" I asked, grabbing the teacup.

"The neutralizer—don't you see?"

I looked into the teacup. "Excuse me?"

"George said he *had* an equalizer," Monty said quickly. "Something powerful enough to stand against a dragon, an enclave of dragons. He didn't use it against us."

"We wouldn't be here talking about it if he had."

"There are few artifacts powerful enough to help someone stand against a dragon. Most of them are locked away in vaults at the sects."

I made the connection. "Oh, shit. The neutralizer?"

"Is currently sitting in Fordey Boutique, unguarded."

"But the security measures?"

"I'm sure they've been compromised by Hekla on her 'visit' to make sure the neutralizer was safe."

"A smash and grab?" I shook my head. "How is George going to get to Fordey? He can't cast."

"I cast runes in front of Hekla, twice," Monty replied. "Once to get to Fordey and once to get her back home. She would know the runic configuration and be able to give them to—"

"Salao, who just used a rift to leave the park. He could get them to Fordey. Hekla was acting?"

"A command performance. I think we're going to need to pay the Jotnar a visit."

"Monty, this sounds like a stretch. I mean, George was clever, and fearless, but he wasn't a tactician," I said, shaking my head. "This is some next-level 'Kasparov seeing thirty moves ahead' kind of planning. George could never do something this intricate. He's a blunt instrument. This is scalpel work."

Monty nodded. "It's sublime in its execution,

each strand tightly wound and plucked just so."

"I think it's great you can admire this wonderful mastermind, but—"

"I don't admire the *person*," Monty said, surprised. "I do, however, admire the complexity of scheme."

"Oh, this is just a professional admiration for the depth of deception and conniving abilities of some individual who wants the neutralizer for…?"

"Whoever or whatever is behind this is planning something much worse than a vendetta against dragons. George's grief has him twisted and they're using him to get to the neutralizer, but why?"

"He's human." It was starting to make sense, but I was still missing some pieces. "He can get close."

"Well obviously, he's human. What does that have to do with any—?"

"No, don't you see? If they're stealing the neutralizer, George doesn't have anything to neutralize," I answered quickly. "He doesn't use magic. Whatever happened to Hekla must be magic-based. She must have told them about the extra layer of defenses."

"Another angle I didn't see. Whoever is behind this is astounding."

"Great, when you meet the schemer you can tell him you're a fan. In the meantime…drakes incoming?"

"We can't have them following us." Monty looked around the mansion. "Especially if we need to get to the boutique."

"Why are you looking around like that? Do I need to remind you that this building is a landmark?"

"If I modify the sphere to create a runic inhibitor, it can boost our energy signatures."

"I'm following you so far, sort of a trap to attract the drakes, right? Once they enter the trap, then what happens?"

"After I simulate the false energy signatures, the drakes will cause the sphere to reach critical mass, forcing it to collapse in on itself in an irreversible cascade, imploding, and destroying them," Monty said with a nod as if he were speaking normal English. "Very similar to exceeding the Chandrasekhar limit for a white dwarf."

"The Chandra who? White dwarf?" I asked, confused. "Did we just venture into astrophysics?"

"Space is the final frontier. Just not the way most think."

I stared at him for a few seconds. "Monty, your brain is a vast and scary place. I just want to know if the mansion survives the imploding part? We do not need the Landmark Commission after us."

"I don't see why not." Monty moved a strand of hair from his face. "The spell would require line of sight, but I can calibrate it to cause minimal damage to the outer structure, diverting all of the energy inward. We, however, need to be clear of this sphere."

"Inward meaning the drakes, not the mansion, right?"

"I thought I just said that?" He straightened his sleeve and gave me the 'why do I bother explaining anything?' look. "Weren't you paying attention?"

"Why do you do that?" I pointed at his sleeves.

"What?"

"That thing you do with your sleeves. It's not like they're shrinking."

"I don't do *anything* with my sleeves. Were you listening to a word I said?"

"I was listening. It's just that sometimes, between your magespeak and astrophysics, my neurons have to realign to keep up. Maybe I just lost too much blood, since George just tried to rearrange my internal organs with a Ka-bar."

"You're fine," Monty said, waving my words away. "I just need to shift the polarity of the sphere to trigger a cascade, and then we can leave."

We moved to the north side of the mansion and looked outside. There was no activity.

"We seem clear for now," I said, looking through a window. "These things don't read like anything we've come up against. So I can't be sure."

"He can," Monty said, pointing at Peaches. "Ask him while I set up the cascade. I need to know when they're in proximity. Then I'll create an opening in the sphere and let them in."

"Will there be another opening for us to get out?"

"That door." He pointed at the north exit. "We'll have about ten seconds before it seals. If I keep it open any longer, the sphere integrity collapses. That would result in an *explosion*, not an implosion. With us in it."

"That sounds like a worst-case scenario. Can't you just drop the energy signature on the floor and lure the drakes in?"

"You really weren't paying attention," he snapped. "I will be doing *exactly* that, but the casting takes work and time. Keep an eye on those drakes. I need to know when they're close."

"No need to bite my head off," I said, moving to the door and looking down at my trusty hellhound. "See? When I drink java, it *improves* my mood. Do you know why? Because I'm not drinking moldy leaf juice."

Monty ignored me, stepped off to the center of the living room, and began forming runes on the floor.

Peaches nudged me, nearly crushing me into the wall.

<Hey, boy. Can you feel any bad men coming? Like before, the ones that stay and go?>

He chuffed and rumbled.

<I feel many of them. They're coming.>

"He says there's a bunch on their way," I called out to Monty, keeping my eyes on the north side while drawing Grim Whisper.

"Can   he   give   you   a   count?   Even   an

approximation would be useful."

"A count, really? I don't think numbers are his strong suit here. Maybe if he were planet-sized Peaches XL I could, but at this size...how exactly would I get a count, in sausages?"

"Droll," Monty said and wiped his brow. "He just needs something to compare against."

"I haven't tried mental imagery. We're just getting the hang of communicating at this point. I don't know if I could give him a picture of a mob of drakes."

"I see. Your bond still needs to mature." Monty gestured and formed a large amount of orbs about half an inch in size. He released them and they floated next to Peaches. "Ask him if it's more or less than that."

<The bad men. Is it more or less than these orbs?>

I pointed to the floating orbs. Peaches' eyes glowed red for a few seconds. He shook his body and chuffed at me.

<Many more than that. But they stay and go.>

I tried counting the floating orbs but they kept moving around, making it impossible.

"Monty, how many orbs did you just create for Peaches to count?"

"Fifty," Monty said, still focusing on the floor. "What did he say?"

"A lot more than fifty, but I think the porting may be throwing off the count." I rubbed Peaches' head. "You almost done?"

"Almost. Bloody hell, more than fifty will be difficult to contain." Monty gestured and placed a palm on the floor, burning a rune into the wood. "That will help with the calibration and regulate the mass-energy input. Get to the door, I'm opening the sphere."

TWENTY-THREE

"TEN SECONDS." I looked out the door. "How far past the sphere do we need to be?"

"Not far," Monty replied. "It's an implosion. We just need to be outside of the sphere. Ready?"

I nodded, and he gestured. A break in the orange field around the house appeared in front of the door. One of Sal's men raced into the mansion from the opposite end, saw Monty, and transformed mid-leap.

The man turned into a half-human, half-dragon, and all flamey creature as it unleashed a fireball from its mouth, forcing Monty to jump back. I fired Grim Whisper from the door, spinning the drake mid-air as the rounds punched into it.

Monty backed up, releasing several orbs, hitting it in the chest, and launching it back several feet before it exploded.

"Are they supposed to do that? Explode on

expiration?"

"I'm not an authority on drakes," Monty said, backing up some more. "However, I suggest you keep your distance before they expire."

"You think?" Through the flames, I could see more drakes approaching. "It's a good thing you said that, I was just about to dive in with Ebonsoul and treat myself to the ultimate flambé experience."

"This would be a good time *not* to use your blade."

"Noted." I backed up and made a mental note to give drakes clearance to avoid getting dragonploded with them when they checked out. "The overwhelming numbers are a bit concerning, Monty. Where are they keeping this many drakes?"

"Excellent question," Monty said, stepping back farther and gesturing. The sphere closed as a drake ran into the energy field and bounced back into the mansion. The howl of screams grew louder as more drakes entered. "That way."

Monty pointed straight back from the mansion and took off at a run. I glanced back to see the interior of the sphere covered in flames before I caught up.

"What happens if they run *around* the mansion?" I asked, as I caught movement on our right.

"You shoot them and keep your distance."

"Okay, just checking." I pivoted to the side, firing, and dropped two drakes that exploded a few seconds later.

"Impressive." Monty turned and faced the mansion.

"Told you I didn't miss." I scanned around the mansion in case there were any more stragglers.

Monty began gesturing, forming orange runes that flared and then faded from sight. The sphere grew brighter and expanded. A few seconds later, I noticed it was still growing.

"I'm pretty sure the word 'implode' implies collapsing in on itself. Why is your sphere growing?"

Monty stopped gesturing and glanced at me. "Bollocks," he said quietly. "We need to get to the car."

"Wait, what do you mean by 'bollocks?'" I said, walking fast and then running to keep up with him. "That bollocks just sounded like 'oops.' Was that an oops? How large is that thing going to get?"

We covered the two blocks in record time. I opened the back door for the hellhound and strapped him down with both seatbelts. Monty jumped in the passenger side, placed a hand on the dash and turned on the engine. Peaches whined from the back, looking at the orange energy obscuring Gracie Mansion from view. I strapped on my seatbelt and looked behind us.

I sat there, transfixed by the sphere. "That thing is huge. Is it still grow—?"

"Simon, drive!"

I floored the gas and raced down 86th Street, away from Carl Schurz Park. I looked in the rearview mirror and noticed the glow from the sphere.

"What happened? You said it was going to implode. That looks like an explosion."

Monty opened the window and crawled halfway out. He began gesturing rapidly. A trail of orange and violet runes shot from his fingers and back to the sphere. After about thirty seconds, he crawled back in, closed the window, and re-fastened his seatbelt.

"I may have made a slight miscalculation," he said, pinching the bridge of his nose. "Bollocks."

"A *slight* miscalculation?" I muttered under my breath as I dodged traffic. "An extra spoonful of sugar in a cup of coffee is a slight miscalculation. Einstein thinking the universe was stable is a slight miscalculation. That thing back there? That is not a *slight* anything!"

He tapped his chin. "Perhaps there was some latent influence from the aura of misfortune? I'm certain I accounted for any variance in the energy output."

"Fantastic, Spock, now in English?" I shot back. "Why are we driving like a bat out of hell?"

"The sphere is going to act like a supernova." Monty glanced back. "It will collapse and then expand, releasing a runic shockwave proportional to the energy contained within."

"Is there a safe distance? What about the people between us and the park?"

"It's a runic shockwave. There may be some destruction, but the real danger will come from the runic component. I don't know what will happen to any magic-user caught in the blast."

"Are we safe in the Dark Goat?"

"I really hope Cecil didn't skimp on the runic protections in this car." Monty looked around the interior. "Still, you may want to drive faster."

I saw the flash in the rear-view mirror followed by the *thwump* of a bass beat on the world's largest drum as the sphere vanished from view. Monty turned.

"What was that?"

"It's collapsing. Can we go faster?"

"The pedal is on the floor. Unless Cecil mounted rockets I don't know about, this is our top speed."

"The wave is approaching. Brace yourself."

I shook my head. "Brace myself? How am I supposed to—?"

A fist of energy slammed into the Dark Goat and lifted us up into the air. A kaleidoscope of runes blazed in the interior as we sailed down 86th Street. Monty was gesturing furiously next to me, his fingers moving too fast to track. White runes surrounded us.

The last thing I remember was doing a barrel

roll and observing the velocity of the street as it raced up at us, before another orange flash blinded me.

TWENTY-FOUR

I LOOKED AROUND and noticed all of the emergency vehicles driving past us. I heard a firm tap. Still dazed, I couldn't connect the sound to the hand I saw on the window. I checked inside. Monty was bleeding from a cut across his brow. Peaches rumbled but kept his gaze fixed on me. Hellhounds were truly indestructible.

<You okay boy?>

<I'm hungry. You need to learn how to use this vehicle. Can we get some meat?>

<I wasn't driving.>

<I know. We rolled on the ground then we hit the wall and other vehicles. Did you forget how to use it? Are you hungry too?>

I opted against discussing driving fundamentals with my hellhound and checked on Monty instead. He seemed unhurt except for the gash across his forehead. Another tap, this time louder, caught my attention.

A man dressed in a dark red uniform with an angry expression on his face was signaling me to open the door. He looked vaguely familiar, but I couldn't place him. I focused and looked closely at his face. He was yelling something when I pushed open the door.

"...the goddamn door, Strong!"

I shook my head again. "Frank?" I noticed the blue, extra-large ambulances parked on the side of the street. More emergency vehicles raced by. My body flushed hot as it healed me.

"How the hell are you still alive?" He undid my seatbelt and pulled me out as more EMTe workers grabbed and gently led me to one of the ambulances. They gave me a short nod, which I returned, and tossed me a bottle of water.

"Thanks," I said, catching the bottle, still semi-dazed. "C'mon, Frank. It was just a small collision."

Frank held my head still and flashed a light in my eyes. "Small collision?" He growled, pointing down the street at the destruction left in our wake. "Judging from the Pontiac-sized crater over there, you collided with the *street*, from about thirty feet up, rolled, and then totaled those three cars over there."

I followed his hand and saw the mangled cars parked on the street. I turned to look at the Dark Goat, expecting to see more of the same damage.

The Dark Goat was untouched. I silently thanked Cecil and refocused on Frank, who grabbed my face and turned my head slowly.

Frank defined grizzled. Older, mid-sixties, built like a wall and probably as tough. He was the oldest EMTe still in the field and was affectionately known as the OG. I thought it meant "old gangsta," but one of the other EMTe told me it meant "original geezer."

"Damn car doesn't even have a scratch on it," Frank muttered giving me a once-over. "What the hell happened?"

"Check Monty. He's injured."

"I'm fine," Monty groaned from inside the Dark Goat. The EMTe backed away from an especially cranky Monty exiting the car. "I *said* I'm fine."

"Take off, I got this," Frank barked at the rookie. I heard some of the other workers laugh under their breath as they jumped in the other ambulance and raced off.

"EMTe" stood for EMT elite. The NYTF used these paramedics whenever they encountered some kind of supernatural disaster, or when Monty was allowed to run rampant, which was pretty much the same thing. They all wore dark red uniforms and drove around in blue, extra-large, rune-covered ambulances.

They were the Navy Seals of the paramedics. Tough as two-day-old steak, and willing to risk their lives no matter the situation. Some of them had magical healing ability, and they all possessed certain 'sensitivities' to supernatural phenomena.

Monty and I had become a widely discussed topic among the EMTe community, given my body's allergic reaction to dying. Most of them took it in stride, giving me space and time to let my body heal itself. Others, the rookies, always tried to help me, only to be shocked when I recuperated before their eyes from something that should have killed me.

It was a small group, and I knew most of them. They always let the rookies try to treat Monty or me as some kind of initiation. It usually ended with either Monty yelling at them or the poor rookie backing away from me in fear.

I looked around. Only Frank's ambulance was on the scene. Not that there was much of a scene. A few totaled cars didn't generate much attention. A squadron of emergency vehicles and EMTe out in force meant something truly Montyesque had happened in the park.

"How did you get here so fast?" I asked. "We just left the park."

"Fast? What time do you think it is?"

I did a mental calculation. We met George at 0600. By the time we were racing down 86th Street and away from Monty's sphere of destruction, only a little more than an hour had passed. We must have been out for some time since Frank was pounding on the Dark Goat after we crash-landed. I added another ten to fifteen minutes just to be safe side.

"Eight a.m.?"

"That was two hours ago, kid." Frank looked away from my shocked expression and down 86th Street. "From 88th to 90th Street, Carl Schurz looks like it's been nuked. You wouldn't happen to know anything about that now, would you?"

"The mansion?" I asked, glancing over at Monty. "Is Gracie Mansion still there?"

"Sure," Frank said. "It's still there."

I breathed out a sigh of relief. "Good. At least it's still in one—"

"It's there and in the East River." He nodded. "I think some of it landed on Roosevelt Island, and one of the first responders swore he saw a part of it in Queens."

"Shit."

"What happened? Or do I not want to know?"

"It's complicated," Monty said.

"It always is with you two. How bad is it?"

Monty and I both remained silent.

"Well, fuck me," Frank said quietly, still looking at the park. "I should've known the quiet wouldn't last. You two had better go do whatever it is you do. I have an emergency to deal with."

He packed up his bag, and I extended my hand. "Thanks, Frank."

"Don't thank me," he said, extending a rough callused hand and grabbing mine. "Stop blowing up my city and go fix whatever it is that needs fixing."

He jumped in the ambulance and sped toward the park.

TWENTY-FIVE

"WE NEED TO get to Fordey." Monty began gesturing. "We've lost hours."

"And Gracie Mansion. You remember—the building we were supposed to *not* explode all over the city?"

"Do you have a special attachment to this Gracie Mansion?" Monty peered at me over the flowing runes. "I'm sure it can be rebuilt."

"I have a special attachment to not being blamed for your slight miscalculations that always seem to contain extenuating circumstances."

"There *were* extenuating circumstances. The aura of—"

"No." I held up a hand. "Not discussing it. I'm sure Ramirez will call me later, chewing me out for destroying Carl Schurz Park. Thanks."

"I'll make sure to take it up with him," Monty suggested. "I'll even make sure we contribute to the cleanup and rebuilding. Right now, we need to get to Fordey, or there won't be a reason to rebuild."

"Point taken." I nodded. "What about the Dark Goat? We can't leave it in the middle of 86th Street. Remember—no valet parking."

"Park it." He turned to the sidewalk and shifted the gesturing. Two cars tumbled onto the sidewalk, creating a large parking spot. "There. I'm opening a rift."

I parked and locked the Dark Goat. White runes drifted from Monty's fingers as he opened a rift.

"I have a feeling this is going to suck."

I stepped into the rift behind Monty, with Peaches by my side. We arrived on the other side and stepped into a cloud of smoke. Small fires blazed around us.

"Are your runes working?" I asked through coughs, covering my face. "Where are we?"

"This is the Hall of the Ten."

We stood in the dim reception area the size of a large hotel lobby. All the white marble benches situated along the wall were in pieces.

I looked around at the craters and missing chunks of wall. Most of the statues were gone or broken. It was a burned-out war zone. I barely recognized it, and even then only because I had seen it prior to it being used as a battleground.

A crater, still smoldering, made up half of what

used to be the large gleaming golden X, which dominated the center of the black marble floor. The domed window set in the ceiling was shattered.

"Do you think LD expanded the Danger Room?" I asked, looking around at the destruction. "Maybe an artifact exploded?"

"I think Fordey was visited by Salao, George, and many drakes." Monty looked around and gestured. "Someone is here but the energy signature is faint. That way."

"What about the neutralizer?"

"I don't sense it. Which means it's either been moved or taken. Our best chance of finding out lies with whoever is still here."

Monty ran down the nearest corridor and stopped short after a few feet, causing me to skid to a stop behind him.

"What happened? Did you forget something?"

"We can't go this way." Monty stepped to the side and let me look down the corridor. "It must be part of the defenses."

Three feet in front of us the corridor shifted left, and a few moments later, it twisted and turned right. It was like looking at Escher's stairs on psychotropic drugs. The corridors defied logic or the laws of physics, twisting and rotating in every direction every couple of seconds.

"What the hell?" I said, looking away before my brain seized. "Now I know why they're called

Corridors of Chaos. There's no way we can walk through that."

"Indeed, we'd be lost in seconds, but we have a way to travel the corridors without becoming irrevocably lost."

"Great," I said. "You have some kind of locator spell that can give us fast travel to this person?"

"I don't. You do."

"You want me to use my Incantation of Light down these corridors?"

"Don't be daft. I want you to use your creature to locate the energy signature of whoever is still here and take us to that person." He looked at me, shaking his head. "Did you seriously suggest your Incantation of Light?"

"Well, you said I had the spell." I crouched down next to Peaches.

"I meant your creature possessed the ability to transport us through these corridors," Monty replied, examining the residue around some of the craters. "When I said you, I was using the royal you. Not you specifically."

"Oh, that's clear as dirt now. Let me see if he can sense this person."

<Hey, boy. Can you feel anyone here?>

<I feel you and the angry man.>

<Okay, that's good. Can you feel anyone else?>

Peaches padded down the corridor a few feet and rumbled before looking back at me.

<The scary lady is here. But she feels quiet.>

<Quiet?>

<Like when I'm going to bite a bad man, I get quiet. Then I can get close.>

<Do you remember when you took Monty and me to the scary lady before? Can you do that again?>

I had no idea if he would remember. It was my experience that most dogs operated in the eternal *now*. Peaches, though, wasn't like most dogs.

<Is she going to make me meat?>

<If you find her and take us to her, I'll make sure she makes you an extra-large sausage.>

<Meat is life. I will take you to her.>

"He said he can do it. Sounds like it may be TK."

"Let's find out why TK would still be here."

Peaches chuffed and stepped back to the edge of the Corridors of Chaos. Monty and I grabbed his collar. The runes around his neck became a bright red, and the corridors disappeared.

TWENTY-SIX

WE REAPPEARED IN a narrow corridor leading
to a large open vault door, easily three feet deep,
covered with dark violet runes. The last time I was
in this corridor, the runes pulsed in time with the
throbbing in my head. This time, they were
dormant. Something had shifted.

Behind the door lay a small, empty, steel room.
In a shallow depression in the center of the floor,
surrounded by ancient symbols I didn't
understand, sat a dark stone vibrating with power. I
was simultaneously drawn to and repulsed by the
stone. As I looked closer at the heart-sized gem, I
noticed that it shimmered in and out of sight as it
pulsed.

Monty stepped close to the depression and
narrowed his eyes. "The Black Heart is still here.
But the neutralizer is gone." He looked around the
room. "I thought your creature sensed an energy

signature? Is it possible he sensed the Black Heart?"

"No, he said the 'scary lady.' The Black Heart isn't a scary lady." I looked around the room. "He also said she was being quiet. Sounded like he meant camouflaged."

Monty narrowed his eyes and scanned the room. He walked quickly to one side of the room and started gesturing.

"Not camouflaged, trapped." He finished gesturing and opened a rift. TK stepped into the room, covered in black energy. "It must have been the aura of misfortune."

"Danger Room. Now," she said and opened another rift. "They took the neutralizer and shunted Fordey sideways. They're leaving through the Danger Room." She stepped through the rift and vanished.

We followed her and arrived at a drake-filled Danger Room. They turned almost as one and snarled at us. I counted at least thirty dragon-men.

"How long ago did they take the neutralizer?" Monty asked, looking around at the angry, snarling faces.

These drakes weren't excited to shred us. I noticed they kept their distance from us…from her.

"I have no way of telling," TK answered under her breath. "When I cast a temporal trap it backfired and caught me. I never miscast. I don't know how you found me, but it's too dangerous to travel the Boutique at the moment. All the defenses are active."

"The aura of misfortune must have affected your cast, trapping you," Monty said. "Why didn't they take the Black Heart?"

"They tried. When I cast the temporal shunt it must have moved Fordey slightly out of their plane."

"Enough to trap you and let them escape."

"You've faced these men before?"

I nodded. "Two of them? One with crazy eyes and one an older, military type carrying an arsenal and a glowing yellow pendant?"

"Yes, and a multitude of drakes," TK added, taking in the room. "Enough to make me consider a Kragzimik is involved, but I didn't see or sense one."

"It appears they left you the multitude of drakes to make sure you didn't follow them," Monty said and flexed his fingers. "We're here to assist."

"Tristan, do you recall the sphere of protection LD taught you? After the Reckoning?"

"Yes, I recently—"

"Cast it, now."

TK stepped forward as Monty pulled me to a corner of the Danger Room. Her eyes must have been awful in a truly old testament sort of way, judging by the way the drakes skittered away.

She gestured with one hand and made a fist with

the other. Monty looked at the symbols she was creating.

"Bloody hell." He looked around at the Danger Room. "We don't have enough room. She's going to cast that thing and kill us all. She's insane."

"What is it? What is she doing?"

"Simon, once I create the sphere, pull up your shield...and pray it's enough."

"Why? Isn't your imploding sphere of miscalculation enough?"

He shot me a glare and began gesturing.

"Do you remember Nana's phoenix fist?"

I nodded, remembering how Dex and I barely made it out alive after Nana unleashed one of those. I made sure I had access to my mala bracelet. "Are you serious? Is the sphere going to be enough?"

"I don't know," Monty said, crouching down to the floor. "She's doing something worse."

"Worse? What's worse than a phoenix fist?" I turned to see him tracing runes fast and placing his hands on different sections of the floor in front of him. Every time he lifted a hand, the faint impression of a rune lingered.

"There's a variation on the spell that makes it exponentially more powerful and almost impossible to control."

"TK is casting that? Why would she do that?"

He glanced at me for a second in between the gesturing.

"Because she can."

"What is she casting? What is this variation?"

The drakes seemed to overcome their initial fear of TK and advanced on her. She leaped into the air. Monty slammed both hands on the floor, creating the orange sphere around us. I pressed my mala bead and materialized my shield. Peaches whined and growled next to me.

TK floated for what seemed an eternity, slowly doing a pirouette. The black energy that covered her body seconds earlier had concentrated around her fist, making it appear like she held a black hole in her hand.

"That"—Monty kept his hands on the floor, and I could see the sweat forming on his face—"is a dark phoenix."

TK's eyes were closed. When she reached her zenith, she turned her body like an Olympic diver, extended her arm, and with an open hand, descended. The drakes turned to face her, opened their mouths, and unleashed a wave of flame orbs.

Black energy blasted out of TK's hand, engulfing the orbs and swallowing them. A beam of black and violet energy punched into the floor. The beam vaporized the drakes closest to TK when she touched the Danger Room floor. A five-foot radius of wood and debris floated lazily up from the floor with TK at its center.

She stood and turned in a slow circle. Green energy arced all over her body to blend with the black and violet. I saw death and pain in her eyes. The outer circle of drakes that survived the initial impact realized the impending destruction in that gaze and scrambled to get away.

It was too late.

TK lowered her head for the span of one heartbeat, and time seemed to stop. She closed her hand into a fist with a blinding violet flash. The floating debris shot out in every direction as the shockwave chewed up the floor, racing outward from the epicenter that was TK.

I looked over the shield at the drakes. The shockwave finished any that weren't caught in the initial blast. It was the same as London when Nana executed the phoenix fist, except this time we were too close to the blast.

The runic shockwave sped across the floor, colliding into Monty's sphere, slowly disintegrating it.

"Monty, your sphere isn't holding up," I said, reinforcing my arm against the wave of energy trying to erase us.

"I'm aware the sphere is failing. Keep that shield up!"

Peaches pulled away from me, increasing in size with each step. His collar glowed white, partially blinding me.

<It's too dangerous, boy! Don't go out there.>

<Neither you nor the mage possess the ability to withstand the force of this wave. Attempting to do so will

result in catastrophic injuries for the both of you. You are my bondmate. I must intervene.>

"Peaches, no!"

"What is he doing, Simon? That wave…is too powerful. Even for him."

"I tried telling him that, but he won't listen."

<You can't do this, boy.>

<I must. This energy level will kill the mage. He is not fully recovered from his encounter with this woman.>

Peaches confirmed what I had thought. Monty had been dragging ever since the Reckoning. Dealing with Salao's drakes, and now this, meant his defenses were nearly gone.

The collar around Peaches' neck shifted hue and changed from white to dark blue. He stepped out from the sphere. He was about SUV-size but hadn't quite reached Peaches XL-size.

He turned sideways and dropped to the floor in front of us, blocking the wave from destroying Monty's sphere, and effectively creating a wall of Peaches. He growled as the shockwave buffeted his body.

Monty removed his hands from the floor and began gesturing. Around us, the sphere began to collapse.

"What are you doing?" I asked, looking around as the wave disintegrated Monty's sphere. "Can't you make it bigger? The sphere won't hold up on its own."

"Neither will your creature," Monty answered,

stepping close to Peaches. Golden runes flowed from his hands and into Peaches' body. "Get your shield over here to block the wave from behind."

"How long does this wave last?" I yelled over the intensity of the blast all around us. Peaches howled but didn't move. "It's hurting him, Monty."

I made a move to reach for my mark.

"No, Simon!" Monty slapped my hand away. "Too many forces are at play. If you introduce another temporal component, we could be trapped."

"It's hurting him." I pulled my hand away from my mark. "We need to stop this wave."

"Not…much longer." Monty put both hands together and bowed his head. I saw him take a breath and yell something I couldn't understand. When he separated his hands, a lattice of orange energy covered Peaches. "There…that should protect him long enough."

Monty stood still for a few seconds and then collapsed. The wave kept raging around us, destroying everything in its path. I dragged Monty with one arm and kept him sandwiched between Peaches and the mala shield.

After what felt like a lifetime, the energy around us suddenly stopped.

<You and the mage are safe. Good.>

<Are you okay? That looked bad. Are you hurt?>

<The lattice of energy provided by the mage helped mitigate much of the damage. I require sustenance to

replenish the expenditure of energy.>

   <Get some rest. I'll make sure to get you some meat.>

   <Meat is life.>

Peaches rolled over on his side with a loud rumble. I jumped back quickly, pulling Monty with me to avoid being crushed by my oversized hellhound. The collar around his neck had become dormant again while the lattice around him pulsed with latent energy.

He chuffed, closed his eyes, and shrank back to normal. I checked to make sure he and Monty were still breathing before I stood and looked across the Danger Room.

TWENTY-SEVEN

TK STOOD IN the center of the floor. All of the drakes were gone, along with most of the floor and sections of the walls.

A cloak of calm fury descended over me as I walked toward her.

"You almost killed them." My voice was hard, full of jagged edges.

"No," TK said, looking around the Danger Room. "I think I got them all. LD is going to have a fit when he sees this place. It's a good thing he went on ahead."

"You're insane," I said, staring at her. "You nearly wiped us all out."

Something in my voice must have caught her attention. TK looked up and cocked her head to one side. A slight smile crossed her lips. "I never said I *was* sane. You're angry? Good."

"Good? How can you stand there saying good?

Your dark phoenix almost erased—"

"Don't think for one second I wasn't aware of the danger," TK interrupted and stared at me. The anger I felt quickly decided it was time to exit the premises. "Where do you think you are? Who do you think you're dealing with? Someone or something powerful facilitated the removal of the neutralizer. From *my* home."

"Salao and George," I shot back. "They were the ones who took it."

TK looked around the Danger Room floor again and shook her head. "No."

"What do you mean no? You said they were the ones who took it."

"They may have taken it, but something is directing their actions. With this many drakes I would swear a Kragzimik was part of the plan. Only they command that many drakes at once."

"That's what Ezra said, but he said it was only rumor."

"Ezra?"

"Old Jewish scholar-looking guy? Has a deli downtown with amazing food?"

She narrowed her eyes at me. "You *know* Azrael?"

I nodded. TK headed over to where Peaches lay. Monty got to his feet slowly.

"She's right, we're not just dealing with Salao and George," Monty said with a groan. "I've never experienced a dark phoenix firsthand. No wonder

Nana never used it. How did you contain it?"

"You can't," TK said, gesturing. Golden runes cascaded onto Monty. "A dark phoenix has to run its course, or the effects can be fatal to the caster."

"They're certainly fatal to everything *around* the caster." I examined the charred remains of the drakes around us.

"It's designed to be that way. There was no way I was going to be able to deal with all those drakes before one hit me with a flame blast. I needed to be fast, efficient, and lethal."

"It's incredibly effective." Monty pulled out one of his mage powerbars from a pocket. I think the flavor was 'freshly tilled soil,' judging from the color. "Excuse me."

"You still haven't recovered from the Reckoning." TK pointed at the powerbar. "Those things taste horrendous."

"They get the job done," Monty said, finishing it off and producing another one from his pocket. "Would you like one?"

"No, thanks. If by 'get the job done' you mean taste like old dirt, then I agree." TK scrunched her face at the mage powerbar. "How long have you known Azrael?"

"For some time now." Monty pocketed the powerbar. "Ezra did mention the possibility of a Kragzimik, but we haven't encountered one."

"You two never cease to amaze. A Kragzimik would never work with a human. They, and all dragons, consider themselves to be a superior species."

"How about a demigod?" I wondered aloud.

"Yes." TK nodded. "They would still consider them inferior, but dragons and demigods have been known to work together, at least for a short time, before turning on one another."

TK crouched and placed her hands on Peaches' side. Golden runes flowed down into his body for several seconds.

"Why would a Kragzimik want the neutralizer?" I asked and rubbed Peaches' head when he stirred. TK gestured again and made a huge sausage for my ever-hungry hellhound, who pounced on it and began chewing.

<This is good meat. Please let her know.>

"My hellhound approves of your magic sausage creating."

TK rubbed Peaches' flanks as he ate. He was going positively soft.

"Dragons only ever want one thing." TK looked at Monty. "You don't remember?"

"Remember what?" I asked as we left the Danger Room. "What is she talking about?"

"Do you remember when we faced Slif?" Monty pulled on his sleeve. "Do you remember her plan?"

"Before or after she skewered and tried to barbecue me?"

Slif's words came back to me: *'We're wiping the slate clean. The Werewolves were just the start. But we will eliminate them all.*"

"Before we brought her down."

"She wanted to eliminate all supernaturals and magic-users, leaving just the dragons to wield magic. She was very particular about you mages not being worthy."

"Do you think this has something to do with William?" Monty turned to TK. "Do you think he found the source?"

"The source of what? What was William looking for?"

"The source of magic," TK replied, her voice pensive. "Directly or indirectly, this has something to do with that. I need to get to the Black Heart."

"The Corridors of Chaos are doing their MC Escher thing. We couldn't get past them without Peaches bringing us here."

TK gestured and opened a rift. "We aren't using the corridors," she said and stepped through. Monty followed. Peaches, sausage in mouth, padded next to me as we entered after them.

TWENTY-EIGHT

THE BLACK HEART room was at full migraine mode. Runes covered every surface of the room. TK gestured, and the power vibrating around us subsided from 'squeeze my brains to a pulp' to 'punch me in the gut' level as we stepped inside.

Pain squeezed the base of my neck, crawling up into my scalp as the dull throbbing of the room got worse. I rubbed my temples to try to alleviate some of the pain, but it didn't help. TK and Monty looked unbothered.

"It's shifted." Monty looked around. TK stepped to the center of the room. "Temporal anomalies?"

TK nodded. "You need to bring the neutralizer back as soon as possible. By removing it from the configuration LD and I setup, the Black Heart will cause planar shifts. Small ones at first, but growing in size."

"Can you anchor it? Prevent the time-skips?"

"For a short time, but it means I have to stay here. You three will need to go after the neutralizer."

"We don't even know where they are," I managed through a haze of pain. "How are we going to find the neutralizer?"

"Tristan can find the neutralizer—it has a specific signature—but you have to act fast. Tristan, if a Kragzimik is involved, you know the outcome. If you can't get the neutralizer back or it's been compromised—"

"Destroy it," Monty said, his voice hard. "Let's hope it doesn't come to that."

"Prepare for the worst and hope for the best." TK began gesturing around the Black Heart, and the ice pick in my brain caught flame, incinerating the inside of my head. "Go find the bastards who stole the neutralizer. Stop them and close the door."

Monty nodded and, thankfully, stepped into the corridor. He looked into the artifact room one last time before TK nodded, and he closed the door.

"What happens if you have to destroy the neutralizer?" The searing pain in my skull had calmed down to mind-numbing agony as we moved down the corridor. "How bad would it be?"

"Think Carl Schurz Park—"

"That's manageable if we can find somewhere deserted—"

"...multiplied by a factor of one million."

I paused to make sure I'd heard him right. "Shit, if that happened, everywhere would be deserted. Nothing would be left."

"Exactly." He gestured and opened a rift. "Let's make sure it doesn't happen."

We reappeared next to the Dark Goat.

"Can you feel where the neutralizer is?"

"Not exactly. I know it's south from here." Monty pointed. "That way."

"What does it feel like?" I unlocked the Dark Goat to the familiar clanging sounds and orange glow of runes across its surface. "What does something neutralized feel like?"

I opened the door for Peaches, who executed a three-point sprawl in one impressive bound. I got behind the wheel and started the engine.

"It's like a void tugging at me." Monty strapped on the seatbelt. "They must have known they couldn't hide it once they removed it from Fordey. If there's a Kragzimik involved, this is when it would reveal itself."

"We need help."

"No."

"Monty, what are you talking about?" I said, surprised. "We need the NYTF, The Dark Council, all of the Elders at the Sanctuary, Dahvina, and the Wordweavers, maybe even Hades if we can get him."

"No. Don't you understand?" Monty pinched the bridge of his nose with a sigh. "If I have to destroy the neutralizer, everyone you just mentioned, with the exception of Hades, would be killed in the blast."

"But it's just us against Bad Luck Sal, George, and maybe a Kragzimik."

"I'm reasonably certain that you and your creature could survive the blast. That just leaves —"

"You."

"That's an acceptable loss in the grand scheme of things," Monty said quietly. "You know, the needs of—"

"Not to me, and I swear if you Spockify me with the whole 'needs of the many outweigh the needs of the few' line, I'll shoot you."

"Very well, it's just my fervent wish that you and your creature live long and prosper."

I groaned as we sped downtown.

TWENTY-NINE

"WE NEED TO find a way to deal with Bad Luck Sal and his Murphy's Law AOE."

"Murphy's Law AOE?"

"You know, everything that could go wrong does and he blasts it in an area of effect. Sounds better than 'aura of misfortune,' don't you think?"

"Not really," Monty said, rubbing his chin. "But you're right. If we can't stop Salao's ability, we won't have a chance against them."

"What if there's a Kragzimik?" I asked seriously. "What are we facing if one is there?"

"If it's in human form he'll be as strong as an Arch Mage, possibly stronger."

"Wonderful," I said, noticing the sun dropping behind the horizon. "And in dragon form?"

"From what I've studied, larger than Slif, and the usual—fireballs, impenetrable dragon-scale skin, oh, and I hear they can wield magic in either form."

"Anything else to add to the list of destruction that makes up a Kragzimik?"

"Yes. Drakes. They can summon drakes. Hundreds upon hundreds of them."

"Any weaknesses? Maybe an aversion to chocolate or muzak?"

"The eyes. If you can penetrate the eyes, both of them, any dragon, including a Kragzimik, can be defeated. They just happen to be the most protected part of its body."

"Well, now I feel extra confident. Why did I ever think we might need help? Are you sure we don't need help?"

"I'm certain," he said, his voice hard. I knew better than to push it any further. "I have the utmost confidence in us. We can do this."

"Or die in the process."

He nodded slowly. "I'm fully prepared for that outcome, Simon."

"Bullshit!" I slammed the wheel and almost caused the Dark Goat to sideswipe a taxicab in sweet revenge. "We are not racing to our deaths, Monty."

He looked out the window.

"I've never faced a Kragzimik, but I'm not exposing my family and friends to this threat. The only reason you're here is because of your curse. Your creature, because I honestly think *nothing* can kill a hellhound. But understand this, Simon. If I thought for a moment that you were at risk, I'd be doing this alone."

"That's it, Monty. Expose *them* to the threat."

"What threat? They are the threat. How would I expose them to themselves?"

"Can you expose Salao and the Kragzimik to the runic neutralizer? Can it be activated somehow?"

"I'd have to get close enough to touch it. Somehow I don't think they'll just let me hold it."

"Let me handle that part. If you can get it, can you activate it?"

"Yes, but it will neutralize all magic in the area, including your curse."

I remained silent for a few seconds. "I'm fully prepared for what that means."

"Whatever the outcome, it's been an honor fighting by your side, Simon."

"Any sappier and I *will* shoot you, Monty. Now, tell me how close we are."

"Over there." He closed his eyes and pointed as we drove by the South Street Seaport. "What's over there?"

"That's Peck Slip," I said, craning my neck to look at where Monty was pointing. "There's nothing there."

Peck Slip was two blocks of empty real estate that had been converted to a plaza type of space, with planters, large stones, and rentable bicycles for the environmentally concerned city dweller. On either side of Peck Slip, developers had transformed the old shipping buildings into upscale lofts and condominiums, making the area a prime location for those working in the financial district.

"There's something there. The Kragzimik."

"Shit, are you certain?"

Monty nodded and began gesturing. "Yes. He knows we're coming."

I got off the FDR and drove north on South Street.

"Maybe we stay in the Dark Goat and run him over a few times?" I said, slowing down. "I mean, it survived your sphere, right?"

"I don't think even Cecil anticipated a Kragzimik." Monty shook his head. "Would you like to take the chance?"

"Not really." I parked the Dark Goat at the entrance to Peck Slip and got out. I left the car unlocked as we walked up the old cobbled street. "Let's go greet Kraggy."

"Kraggy?"

"There's no way I'm calling him Kragzimik. Are you kidding? Kraggy it is."

"I'm still wondering how you intend to get the neutralizer."

At the intersection of Front Street and Peck Slip stood a lone figure. Peaches rumbled beside me and entered 'maim and obliterate' mode. We approached the figure and I could sense the unnatural signature of drakes all around us.

"The Montague and Strong Detective Agency," the man said in a deep voice. "I've heard so much about you."

"You should really follow us on Facebook. We have an excellent group called the Mages of Badassery," I said, keeping my gaze wide. I noticed Salao and George approaching from opposite sides of the street.

"Simon," Monty said under his breath, "do we want to start with antagonizing the powerful dragon?"

"My associate just made a valid point. You aren't a mage or a badass." I turned to Monty. "Maybe we could create a new group? Dragon Assholes? It could have one member—Kraggy over here."

"Simon," Monty hissed, "this is a bad idea."

"Who has the neutralizer? Can you sense it?"

"Who do you think has it?" Monty looked straight ahead at the Kragzimik. "They must have just given it to him."

"Perfect," I said under my voice, and then louder, "Bring it, Kraggy!"

"Kraggy?" the man said and looked at Salao. "Kill this impertinent *human*."

Salao raced at us. George wasn't too far behind. I ran at them and waved as I ran past them. They were moving too fast to stop and course correct before I got to Kraggy.

I pressed my mark and hoped Karma was taking a vacation. White light shot out from the top of my left hand and everything came to a stop slightly out of focus.

The smell of lotus blossoms wafted by my nose, the scent laden with citrus and mixed with an enticing hint of cinnamon. This was followed by the sweet smell of wet earth after a hard rain.

"Shit."

"You and your friends kept me busy in London," said a voice behind me.

It was Karma.

"You're welcome?"

I turned and braced myself in case she felt like sharing one of her slaps of steel. She was dressed in a black leather power suit, only the bottom was a mini-skirt instead of pants. Leather knee-boots with the word BITCH etched into the sides gleamed in the street lights.

"It wasn't a compliment, Splinter." She was doing 'severe librarian' and wore her hair in a tight bun along with a thin pair of glasses. "Is that a Kragzimik?"

I nodded, still expecting one of her jaw-cracking greetings. She grabbed me by the face and squeezed. I saw stars and my vision tunneled in before she let go. Her hazel eyes gleamed, daring me to stare back. She looked female, but Karma was the personification of causality. I risked madness looking into those eyes for too long.

"Yes, I think he's trying to eliminate magic-users and supernaturals."

"You're getting closer," she said and tapped my cheek, causing stars to bloom in my vision, again. "How is he going to do it?"

"The neutralizer. He plans to strip magic-users of their ability."

"Boring," Karma said, sitting on one of the large stones. "You're a detective. Do better."

I let the facts sift through my brain.

"Kraggy used Bad Luck Sal to convince George to attack the dragons and get the neutralizer, but he *is* a dragon."

"Which means?" She tapped the top of her knee.

"George doesn't know Sal is working for a dragon. This explains why drakes aren't trying to shred us now."

"Why does the Kragzimik want the neutralizer?"

"It's not to strip the magic-users of magic."

"Go further." Karma shook her head and stared at me. "This is a dragon."

"He wants to strip magic...period."

She gave me a smile that chilled my blood and made me take a step back in fear.

"Well done, Splinter." She gave me a golf clap and stood. "Now you're starting to see the picture."

"Can he?"

"Can he what?"

"Remove magic?"

She looked over at the Kragzimik and tapped

her chin.

"I don't know. Do you plan on letting him try?"

"No, I need the neutralizer, and he has it."

"Had it," she said, pointing at my hand. A blue crystal about the size of a golf ball shone in my palm. "How did you? Why?"

"Reasons," Karma said. "Just remember, not everyone is subject to the construct or absence of time."

"What does that mean?" I pocketed the neutralizer.

"You don't always have ten seconds, Splinter." Karma walked away and disappeared.

I headed to Monty, who was down the street, when a searing pain blossomed in my right side. I looked down to see a blade protruding from my side.

"Mr. Strong," Kragzimik said while removing the blade, "you have something that belongs to me."

I drew Grim Whisper and fired. My rounds never reached him. Time was still stalled. He grabbed me by the neck and started to squeeze.

"How can you move through time?" I managed between gasps.

"An insignificant flea like you would never understand the intricacies of the power I wield. Time, as you understand it, is a primitive construct."

He flung me forward and I bounced painfully

next to Monty and the incoming Salao and George.

"This is why you want to remove magic? You think only you deserve to wield it?"

Kragzimik raised an eyebrow. "Impressive." He stepped on my chest, crushing ribs. "Even stupid beasts can have momentary epiphanies, I suppose. Magic and its use is for me and my kind. It has been this way for eons."

"Thanks, Kraggy," I wheezed, wondering how long ten seconds was in dragon pain-land. "That clears it all up."

He punched me in the face. The coppery taste of blood filled my mouth. There was no hot flash, no repair of the cuts and bruises. My curse didn't work outside of time.

"I'm literally out of time." I laughed to myself.

"You find this funny? You see your human friend, George?" He grabbed my hair and turned my head to face George. "He's going to die knowing he helped the very creatures he detests. Once I erase all magic, we will address the hybrid abominations, like this one."

He twisted my head to face Salao.

"He's a demigod, and he helped you," I managed after spitting some blood.

"He's an abomination, and he served my purpose. I allowed him to serve a greater cause than his petty existence."

I tried to speak but found myself short of breath. "Are all dragons," I said in between wheezes, "such monumental assholes?"

He smiled, and I knew the end was close. "Aren't you wondering why you haven't returned?" Kragzimik asked with a sneer.

"Now that...that you mention it, the question has crossed my mind."

He pulled me close. "I'm going to keep you in here until you breathe your last breath. Once you're gone, I'm going to kill your upstart mage friend and the mongrel. Then I'll start with the mutations. Vampires, werewolves, and any supernatural creature that contain even a sliver of magic will be neutralized."

"Sounds like a busy week."

He tightened his grip around my neck, causing me to choke. "As long as you're alive, you will be in here with me. I will take your life in the smallest of measures, savoring each moment."

I still had the neutralizer in my pocket. If I knew how to activate it, I would. Instead, I would have to settle for the next best thing.

Kraggy shoved me back, and I landed next to Monty. I got to my feet shakily and stumbled, leaning on the frozen Monty to remain upright.

"That's what I figured. Just wanted...wanted to make sure." I was going to take a chance. If I timed it wrong, it was the last chance I would take.

I drew Ebonsoul and Kragzimik laughed. "Your blade can't even scratch me."

"I know. It's not for you," I said, plunging

Ebonsoul into my chest.

THIRTY

TIME SNAPPED BACK into place. Monty looked down and saw the neutralizer in his hand. I had placed it there when I leaned on him for support.

"Kill them!" I heard Kragzimik yell. "Get me the neutralizer!"

"Tag, you're it," I managed before falling back. Peaches rushed to my side.

<You're hurt.>

<Keep Monty safe. Make sure the bad men don't get to him.>

<You said stay away.>

<When you see the blue flash, you bite them all.>

<All?>

<Every single one, boy. Don't let one get away.>

<I will be ready.>

I was tired and my body flushed with heat, I knew it was too little too late. Ebonsoul wasn't a normal blade. Plunging it into my chest severed the time loop Kragzimik had created. The only downside was the 'plunging it into my chest' part.

Monty raised the neutralizer and yelled some words I couldn't understand. The blue crystal blazed in his hand, converting night into day for several seconds. I had to close my eyes against the light.

<Now, boy! Get them!>

Peaches winked out, but I didn't see where he winked back in, hopefully around Kraggy's neck. The thought made me smile. I heard the drakes begin to fill the street.

"Sal, what the hell are those things doing here?" George asked, firing at the drakes. "You set me up?"

"You stupid *human*, of course I used you. I only needed you for the neutralizer." Salao extended a hand and unleashed a flame orb. It punched through George's armor and George, knocking him back. "That is better than you deserved."

Salao turned and focused on Monty.

I pulled out Ebonsoul. I may have been going out, but I wasn't going to die on my back. A pair of rough hands grabbed me under the armpits and dragged me closer to Monty.

I started to struggle, trying to get away, but I couldn't get leverage. Whoever had a hold on me had a grip of iron.

"Quit your kicking lad, or I'll feed you to the

drakes," said a familiar voice. "I told my mule-headed nephew to call me *before* you engaged the dragons. Didn't I say it before? I said if you find an enclave, you call me first... *first.*"

"Uncle Dex? How did you get here?"

"And what did I say about demigods? I gave you clear instructions, the both of ye!"

I knew he was upset when his speech started getting old Englishy.

"We didn't want to expose any of you to danger."

"Oh, and the three of you were going to handle a Kragzimik, a demigod, and an army of drakes on your own, were ye?"

"We had a plan." I saw Monty blasting drakes in every direction. Peaches had reached Kragzimik, who remained in human form, probably from the neutralizing blast. Both of them were circling each other.

"Your plan was what?" Dex growled, looking around. "Last ten minutes, then die?"

"A little longer than that, maybe twenty. Dex?"

"What!" he snapped and gestured, flooding my body with golden runes. I was feeling better by the second.

"How did you get here? And did you bring help?"

"I'm a Montague and, unlike my proud nephew, I know when to bring an army. Let's go, boys!"

A deafening roar went up into the night. It didn't

sound like drakes, but I wasn't certain they were friendly either. That's when I saw a sight that confirmed I had lost too much blood. Hundreds of tigers leaped off the FDR and onto the street below. They tore into the drakes, rending them to pieces all around us. I managed to get to my feet just as Kristman Dos approached Dex.

"We got the drakes, go put down the dragon."

"Aye, Salao is roaming about," Dex answered. "He was in the neutralizing blast. Why not give him a taste of his own medicine? We need him alive though."

"I'll make sure he runs into some bad luck of his own." Kristman nodded, looked around, and made some signals with his hands. I saw a group of ten tigers peel off from the main group and target Salao. He was going to have some serious bad luck.

"Where's the neutralizer?" LD's voice came from behind me. "We need it now, or all this is for nothing."

"Monty has it." I pointed to his location and LD was gone, only to reappear next to Monty. He was gone again a second later. Roars from behind made me turn.

Peaches had reached planet size, which normally dwarfed everything around him, except this time he was facing Kragzimik, who was no longer in human form.

Kragzimik had grown, considerably. His teeth

were easily the size of my arms. His claws, which raked grooves in the cobblestones, were the size of small cars as he stretched his body along the street. He narrowed his yellow eyes and shook his body, which was covered in black scales tinged with red.

I looked up and resisted the urge to turn and run away screaming. My opinion hadn't changed. Dragons—up close—were truly, unmistakably, petrifying.

The dragon raked Peaches across the side and whacked him with its tail, sending Peaches across the street.

Monty ran up to my side. He was looking a bit rough as he gestured and formed several white-hot orbs.

Dex formed a wall of orbs and grinned at Monty.

"What are you waiting for? You plan on living forever!"

Dex rushed at Kragzimik. Several large groups of weretigers, more than I could count, joined him and Monty. I felt the ground tremble and a cloud of sausage breath enveloped me, making me choke.

<BONDMATE, IT IS TIME TO STOP THE DRAGON. ARE YOU HEALED?>

I winced at the XL voice in my head and nodded. I remembered Monty's advice about weaknesses.

<The eyes, boy. We need to get to its eyes.>

We raced at the Kragzimik. I grabbed Peaches' collar and we blinked out. We blinked back in mid-air over Kraggy and fell.

<The eyes are not up this high.>

<THE DRAGON WILL LOOK UP SHORTLY. YOU WILL HAVE YOUR OPPORTUNITY.>

Peaches' eyes glowed red and he unleashed his omega beams on the Kragzimik, who looked up.

<NOW, BONDMATE.>

<Now, what? You want me to dive into the dragon's face?>

<PUNCTURE THE EYE WHILE IT IS OTHERWISE DISTRACTED.>

I angled my body toward the Kragzimik who whipped his tail around and caught me in the midsection. I bounced on the street for a few seconds before rolling to a stop.

I was about to get up when a hand grabbed my shoulder. I whirled with Ebonsoul, ready to perforate whatever grabbed me, when I saw it was George.

"You look like shit, George. Maybe you should sit this one out."

"I'm sorry, Strong." He reached under his armor and pulled out a long faintly glowing device covered in runes. "Let me make this right."

"What the hell is that?"

He gave me a grin and coughed, spitting up blood.

"Synthetic entropy bomb. My dragon contingency plan, keyed to my energy signature. I just need to get close."

I held out my hand. "We can do it. You're in no condition to get near that thing."

"No, I saw what you just did. Your hound dropped you over it. I can do that. You just need to distract it long enough for me to get close. Besides, *I'm* the detonator."

"It's too risky. If it sees you…it's over."

"Then make sure it doesn't see me. I need to do this, Strong. For Cassandra, for me. Please. Let me make it right. I'll plant it and get clear."

We both knew that was a lie. He wasn't planning on getting clear of anything.

"There's another way. There has to be."

"You know there isn't. Look, I can do this. You owe me, Strong."

Kragzimik was holding his own against Dex and Monty, throwing up shields and countering their spells with blasts and orbs of his own. The weretigers attacked relentlessly, but the dragonscale proved to be too much, even for them. Every few seconds, Kragzimik would swat a handful away from his body. They couldn't keep that up all night.

Periodically, Kragzimik would cast and more drakes appeared, keeping the majority of the weretigers engaged. George was right, we needed to shift the balance of this fight. End it, if possible.

"Goddammit," I cursed under my breath, and George smiled. "You wait for my signal before you launch, you got it?"

"Wait for your signal," he said and grabbed my arm. "Thank you, Strong."

<I need you here, boy.>

Peaches XL appeared a second later.

<The same thing you did with me, I want you to do with him.>

<A FALL FROM THAT HEIGHT WILL PROVE FATAL AND HE IS CRITICALLY INJURED.>

<I know. He has a device that can stop the dragon. He's the only one who can do it. It's keyed to his energy signature.>

<HE WILL NOT SURVIVE THE FALL WITH HIS INJURY. IN ADDITION, HE IS NOT A MAGE NOR WIELDS MAGIC. ANY DEVICE KEYED TO HIS ENERGY SIGNATURE WILL USE LIFE FORCE, FURTHER DECREASING HIS CHANCES OF SURVIVAL.>

<I think that's the plan, boy. Take him up.>

<VERY WELL.>

They blinked out a second later.

THIRTY-ONE

I RAN TO where Monty stood firing orbs at the dragon.

"We need to get and keep its focus on us," I said, firing Grim Whisper.

"Do tell," Monty said, unleashing a barrage of orbs at the dragon. "What did you think I was doing?"

"We need a void vortex," I said, my voice hard.

"Are you insane?" He shook his head. "Do you see how many weretigers are around us? They'll die."

"Not a real one. Kraggy needs to think it's real. Can you do that?"

"And what are you going to do? Convince it to surrender?"

Dex looked up into the night sky.

"Bloody hell, we can do it, lad."

Dex began gesturing and Monty joined him.

Most of the weretigers were busy with the drakes. Kragzimik looked down and laughed.

"You would sacrifice your pitiful lives and this insignificant city in a failed attempt to stop me?"

He unleashed a flame blast. I pressed the main bead on my mala bracelet, materializing my shield, and deflected the blast away.

<Now, boy!>

Dex and Monty kept gesturing and I noticed a corsolis take shape near Kragzimik. How they created one while starting a void vortex made me wonder, but I couldn't focus on it for long.

A black vortex started forming around Kragzimik. It started to take shape, and then it collapsed. I saw Monty and Dex back away, slowly at first, and then run. Kragzimik looked down at me and laughed.

"Run, vermin!" He looked around, gestured, and summoned more drakes. "There is nowhere to hide. Only now at the end, do you understand."

"You're right," I said. "You're too powerful for us."

I saw George land on Kragzimik's head and started backing away. I noticed all of the weretigers had cleared away.

"Cower before me! I am your rightful ruler! What are you?" Kragzimik looked up and tried to swat George off. "Begone, insect. How dare you?"

George gave me a nod and closed his eyes. A white flash filled the sky a second later. Kragzimik screamed as the entropy bomb undid his body.

I ran and felt the energy wave gain ground on me. The ground started shaking, and I realized it wasn't because of the entropy bomb. Peaches was keeping pace next to me.

<YOU DO NOT POSSESS THE SPEED TO OUTRUN THE ENCROACHING ENERGY, BONDMATE. GRAB MY COLLAR.>

I grabbed hold of his collar, and we blinked out. We reappeared about ten blocks away with everyone else.

Monty stepped close to me as I looked at the glowing stream of energy shooting skyward. "In the end, he obtained what he wanted."

I nodded. "I hope he finally found some peace."

Monty nodded and walked over to where Dex and Kristman Dos stood coordinating the weretigers. I looked around and realized I hadn't seen Bad Luck Sal since the pack of tigers had targeted him. I walked over to where the others were.

"What happened to Sal?" I asked.

"My tigers said he just disappeared," Kristman Dos answered. "We have his scent. If he shows up anywhere, I'll know."

"I have a feeling we're not done with that one," Dex said, looking into the night. "I best be heading out as well. The Elders don't know I'm gone."

"Dex, I'll see you soon." Kristman raised a hand and signaled to the streak. "Thank you for the hunt."

"Aye, thank you for the assist." Dex gave him a short bow. Monty and I did the same.

Kristman Dos took a few steps and transformed into one of the largest tigers I'd ever seen. He roared once. The streak echoed the roar and faded into the night. He gave us a nod and bounded off silently after them.

A few seconds later, Dex opened a rift.

"Nephew, remember this night," Dex said, grabbing Monty by the shoulder. "Those who stand beside you when things go well are friends and comrades. Those who stand by your side when it's all gone to shite, are your family. I expect to see you both at the Sanctuary soon."

Dex stepped through the rift and disappeared.

THIRTY-TWO

A FEW DAYS later, we sat in a Haven examination room.

"It's an effect of the proximity to the neutralizer when you unleashed the blast," Roxanne said after looking down at her charts. "How close were you again?"

"It was in my hand," Monty growled. "I cast without difficulty after the blast. Why would this happen?"

"You were still recovering from the Reckoning and dealing with Salao," TK said from the corner. "This would be a good time to relax, maybe go on a vacation."

"A vacation?" He narrowed his eyes at us. "My casting ability has been compromised, and you want me to take a vacation?"

"Rest would be the best thing for you," Roxanne added. "If you don't want to leave the city you can do a staycation."

Roxanne reached into her pocket, pulled out a phone, and stepped out of the room, holding up a finger in our direction.

"That sounds worse than an actual vacation." Monty rubbed his chin. "I suppose I can get in some practice with the Sorrows and brush up on some study."

"That's the attitude, *hombre*. Make the most of it. Look at me." LD shrugged and glanced at TK. "I have to rebuild the entire Danger Room because my lovely wife decided to go all dark phoenix on it."

"There were extenuating circumstances," TK said. "Besides, it needed to be redone after the Reckoning. You kept complaining about the extra entrances. Now you can start from scratch."

"Were you able to secure the neutralizer?"

"Mostly." TK looked at LD. "We had to reconfigure the bridge in a hurry and may have shunted our plane over somewhat."

"Not much," LD said quickly. "Less than one degree. I think."

"The entire plane?" I asked. "What do you mean you *think*?"

"It's not a big deal and should autocorrect over time." LD waved his hand. "Shouldn't take more than one or two millennia. Besides, it only affected runic alignments. Everything else should be fine."

"What does that mean? In English?"

"Oh, only high-level individuals with magic," TK said. "Wizards, mages, sorcerers etc. They may not be where you remember them."

"You trapped them?" I asked, shocked. "We need to get them out."

"No, no. It's not like that." LD raised a hand "They aren't trapped. We're the ones who moved."

"How much? Does that mean we're trapped?"

"Our plane just shifted over a jump to the left." LD held his index and thumb up, almost touching.

"And maybe a step to the right." TK nodded. "It's really difficult to pinpoint these things when dealing with runic quantum units."

"Listen," LD said, putting a hand on my shoulder, "you know how there was a"—he glanced over at a scowling Monty—"wizard in Chicago and another in St. Louis?"

I nodded. "Yes, they're pretty well known. Are they okay?"

"Perfectly fine," LD said, nodding his head. "They just aren't there anymore. At least not for us."

"What?"

"Tristan, you try and explain it to him." LD threw his hands up. "It was just a temporal planar shift. They're in their dimension and we're in ours. Due to the neutralizer configuration, the Black Heart shifted us over just a smidge. It won't realign for a few planar cycles. We need to get back and run some more tests."

Peaches nudged my leg, nearly giving me whiplash.

<Can you have the scary lady make some magic meat?>
<Let me ask.>

"TK, could I trouble you to make some sausage for my bottomless pit of a hellhound?"

"I'd love to." She gestured and formed an enormous sausage that appeared next to Peaches. "Here, let me show you the gesture and rune for that one."

She took my hand and traced the rune. Then she taught me the gesture and had me repeat it until I could do it easily.

"That's it?" I asked, surprised at how easy it seemed. "I thought it would be harder."

She nodded. "It is. Practice, and remember that you have to infuse it with energy or it will taste horrible and your hellhound may bite *you*."

"We need to go." LD opened a rift and looked at Monty. "Take some time to relax. You earned it."

"In the meantime, I hear Azra—Ezra gives obedience lessons to hellhounds." TK bent over and scratched Peaches behind the ears. "Why not get yours some lessons?"

"Sounds like a good idea. Thank you for everything."

"We'll see you soon." LD stepped through the rift and disappeared.

"Tristan, these lulls in power usually happen before a shift. Hone your non-magical skills.

Prepare and sharpen. I doubt that's the last we've heard of dragons."

"I shall, and thank you."

TK nodded and stepped through the rift.

Roxanne stepped back into the room, her face grim.

"Tristan, you have a call." She pointed to the phone on the table next to him.

Monty picked up the room phone. The person on the other end said a few words I couldn't make out and hung up.

"Who was that?"

"Master Yat."

"Master Yat? Is he in town? Can we get some lessons while he's visiting?"

"It wasn't that kind of call," Monty said, leaning back in the bed. "He's in trouble and needs our help."

"There goes the staycation." I looked at Roxanne, who wasn't pleased. "When?"

"Now. He's waiting downstairs."

THE END

CAST

ANGEL RAMIREZ-DIRECTOR of the NYTF and friend to Simon Strong. Cannot believe how much destruction one detective agency can wage in the course of one day.

Cassandra Rott- Daughter of George Rott. Lieutenant in the NYTF under Director Angel Ramirez.

Castor and Pollux-Demigod twins, owners of Hybrid an exclusive hotel that caters to demigods in Manhattan.

Cecil Fairchild-Owner of SuNaTran and close friend of Tristan Montague. Provides transport for the supernatural community and has been known to make a vehicle disappear in record time.

Dex Montague-Uncle to Tristan, brother to Connor. One of the most powerful mages in the Golden Circle.

George "Rottweiler" Rott- Retired NYTF

Special Ops leader of Shadow Company. Father of Cassandra Rott.

Grey Stryder-one of the last Night Wardens patrolling the city and keeping the streets safe. Current owner of *Kokutan no ken*.

Kali-(AKA Divine Mother) goddess of Time, Creation, Destruction, and Power. Cursed Simon for unspecified reasons and has been known to hold a grudge. She is also one of the most powerful magic-users in existence.

Karma-The personification of causality, order, and balance. She reaps what you sow. Also known as the mistress of bad timing. Everyone knows the saying karma is a…some days that saying is true.

Kragzimik-Ancient type of dragon whose purpose is to rid the world of non-dragon magic-users. Much like every dragon. Really despises mages and magic-users.

Kristman Dos-Weretiger leader of the Eastern Streak, a large group of weretigers on the Eastern Seaboard of the United States.

LD Tush Rogue Creative Mage, husband to TK Tush. Proprietor of Fordey Boutique. One of the Ten.

Michiko Nakatomi-(AKA 'Chi' if you've grown tired of breathing) Vampire leader of the Dark Council. Reputed to be the most powerful vampire in the Council.

The Morrigan-Yes *that* Morrigan. Chooser of the Slain and currently in a relationship with Uncle

Dex...don't ask. Also goes by Badb Catha the 'Boiling One.'

Nana-Powerful sorceress and Tristan Montague's first instructor and nanny.

Noh Fan Yat- Martial arts instructor for the Montague & Strong Detective Agency. Teacher to both Simon and Tristan. Known for his bamboo staff of pain and correction.

Peaches-(AKA Devildog, Hellhound, Arm Shredder and Destroyer of Limbs) Offspring of Cerberus and given to the Montague & Strong Detective Agency to help with their security. Closely resembles a Cane Corso-a very large Cane Corso.

Professor Ziller Mage responsible for the safeguarding of the Living Library and the Repository of knowledge at the Golden Circle. Don't try to have conversation with him...it will just melt your brain.

Roxanne DeMarco-Director of Haven. Oversees both the Medical and Detention Centers of the facility. Is an accomplished sorceress with formidable skill. Has been known to make Tristan stammer and stutter with merely a touch of his arm.

Salao-Demigod son of Jyeshtha and a mortal. Possesses the ability to create an aura of misfortune around him.

Simon Strong-The intelligent (and dashingly handsome) half of the Montague & Strong

Detective Agency. Cursed alive into immortality by the goddess Kali.

TK Tush Rogue Creative Mage, wife to LD Tush. Proprietor of Fordey Boutique. One of the Ten. She's not angry...really.

Tristan Montague- The civilized (and staggeringly brilliant) half of the Montague & Strong Detective Agency. Mage of the Golden Circle sect and currently on 'extended leave' from their ever-watchful supervision.

Wordweavers- An ancient sect of magic-users. They manipulate magic through speech and special words of power. Considered to be the first magic-users.

ORGANIZATIONS

FORDEY BOUTIQUE- ARTIFACT specialty store dealing in rare magical items that are usually dangerous and lethal, like the owners

New York Task Force-(AKA the NYTF) a quasi-military police force created to deal with any supernatural event occurring in New York City.

SuNaTran-(AKA Supernatural Transportations) Owned by Cecil Fairchild. Provides car and vehicle service to the supernatural community in addition to magic-users who can afford membership.

The Dark Council-Created to maintain the peace between humanity and the supernatural community shortly after the last Supernatural War. Its role is to be a check and balance against another war occurring. Not everyone in the Council favors peace.

The Ten-A clandestine group of magic-users and shifters whose purpose is to…well that's secret now isn't it?

<u>Special Mentions for Dragons & Demigods</u>

Isabel who showed me how strong George is **every day**.

Tammy-because her eyes must have been awful in a truly old testament sort of way, judging by the way people skittered away.

Larry. Because you refuse to be owned, but you can be rented…LOL.

Craig Z. Who just wanted to make an appearance in a book and be crushed, there you go…you're welcome lol.

To JPL for pointing out the TEA in team!

Darren M. because you wanted running gods…

MaryAnn, Mary Anne, and Lesley who threatened me with tea, plain old tap water and finally settled on hose water that's been sitting in the sun for three hours if I didn't pick up the pace. I'm writing FASTER!!

AUTHOR NOTES

THANK YOU FOR reading this story and jumping back into the world of Monty & Strong. We all know rationally that death is a part of life. This doesn't mean it makes it easier to deal with when it touches our lives or the lives of our loved ones.

This story allowed me to explore those times when we suddenly lose someone near to us, and the feelings that accompany that loss. Thank you for allowing me to deal with those feelings when I wrote this story.

With each book, I want to introduce you to different elements of the world Monty & Strong inhabit, slowly revealing who they are and why they make the choices they do. If you want to know how they met, that story is in NO GOD IS SAFE, which is a short explaining how Tristan and Simon worked their first case.

There are some references you will understand and some...you may not. This may be attributable to my age (I'm older than Monty or feel that way most mornings) or to my love of all things sci-fi and fantasy. As a reader, I've always enjoyed finding these "Easter Eggs" in the books I read. I hope you do too. If there is a reference you don't get, feel free to email me and I will explain it... maybe.

You will notice that Simon is still a smart-ass (deserving a large head smack) and many times he's clueless about what's going on. He's also acquired his first spell (an anemic magic missile!) even though he needs some practice with it. He's slowly wrapping his head around the world of magic, but it's a vast universe and he has no map.

Bear with him—he's still new to the immortal, magical world he's been delicately shoved into. Fortunately he has Monty to nudge (or blast) him in the right direction.

Each book will reveal more about Monty & Strong's backgrounds and lives before they met. Rather than hit you with a whole history, I wanted you to learn about them slowly, the way we do with a person we just met—over time (and many large cups of DeathWish Coffee).

Thank you for taking the time to read this book. I wrote it for you and I hope you enjoyed spending a few more hours getting in (and out of) trouble with Tristan and Simon.

If you really enjoyed this story, I need you to do me a **HUGE** favor— **Please leave a review**.

It's really important and helps the book (and me). Plus, it means Peaches gets new titanium chew toys, besides my arms, legs, and assorted furniture to shred. And I get to keep him at normal size(most of the time).

We want to keep Peaches happy, don't we?

CONTACT ME:

I REALLY DO appreciate your feedback. Let
me know what you thought by emailing me at:
www.orlando@orlandoasanchez.com
For more information on Monty & Strong...
come join the MoB Family on Facebook!
You can find us at:
Montague & Strong Case Files.
To get **FREE** stories visit my page at:
www.orlandoasanchez.com

Still here? Amazing! Well, if you've made it this
far—you deserve something special!

Included is the first chapter of the next
Montague & Strong story,

DRAGONS & DEMIGODS here for you to read.

Enjoy!

Bullets & Blades

A Montague and Strong Detective Agency Book 7

"I don't believe an accident of birth makes people sisters or brothers. It makes them siblings, gives them mutuality of parentage. Sisterhood and brotherhood is a condition people have to work at. "– Maya Angelou

"When brothers agree, no fortress is so strong as their common life."– Antisthenes

ONE

"NOW?" WHAT DO you mean now?" I asked.

"Now." Monty looked at Roxanne. "As in, where are my clothes?"

Roxanne pointed to the suit hanging in the closet on the other side of the room. The energy coming off her was a clear indicator she was displeased.

"Tell him you can't." Roxanne crossed her arms and stared at Monty. "You can't cast. I'll tell him if you won't."

"He's in trouble." Monty got out of bed and got dressed. "I have to help him."

"How?" The energy around Roxanne crept up a notch along with the volume of her voice. "You *can't* cast, Tristan."

Peaches rumbled next to my leg.

<I know, boy. She can be scary.>

<If I lick her, she will calm down. My saliva has

healing properties.>

I forced myself to keep a straight face.

<How about you save that for later, when she doesn't look like she wants to blast Monty?>

<Can you make magic meat yet?>

<Working on it.>

<Good. I'm hungry.>

<When aren't you?>

<When I'm asleep.>

"Mages are trained to be effective even without magic," Monty answered, his voice taking on an edge. "Besides I still have access to my magic and the Sorrows."

"Monty—?" I started. He gave me a look that said his mind was set. "Nevermind. Let's go see him."

"At the very least, take this"—Roxanne removed a brooch and affixed it to Monty's jacket—"that way I know you'll be safe."

Monty looked down at the pendant and shook his head slowly. I looked over and admired the new accessory with an approving eye. It was a round red and silver Celtic design surrounding a trinity knot in the center.

"I have a shieldbearer," Monty said. "*You* should be wearing this."

"Inside Haven I don't need that many layers of protection."

"That's pretty and really brings out the color in your eyes, Monty." He shot me a glare. "What does it do?"

"It's called a bloody bloom and creates a personal shield." Roxanne adjusted it on Monty's jacket. "It won't stop everything, but it's better than nothing. Which is what you have right now—no offense, Simon."

"None taken. Does it come with matching earrings?"

"We need to go." Monty grabbed her hands gently as she adjusted the brooch. "I'll be fine."

"That's what worries me." Roxanne squeezed his hands and looked at me. "You keep him safe."

I nodded. "He has me and my trusty, bottomless hellhound. We'll keep the destruction to a minimum, promise."

Roxanne crouched down and rubbed Peaches' head. "Simon, if his enemies find out he can't cast —"

"I know. I'll keep him safe."

"I'm perfectly capable of keeping myself safe, thank you."

Monty headed out of the room and to the elevators at the end of the corridor. I was about to follow, when Roxanne grabbed my arm.

"He is an obdurate, insufferable mage."

"You forgot slightly insane, tea-addicted and short-tempered. Also prone to massive acts of destruction, should I go on?"

She shook her head with a sad smile. "Bring him back to me, Simon. He holds my heart."

I grew serious and looked down at Peaches. "We'll keep him safe."

I heard the elevator chime and Monty gave me a look, which meant 'wrap it up or I'm leaving you' as he entered the car.

I half-jogged down the corridor and got in the car. Peaches bounded in next to me and I heard a creaking sound as he got in.

<*You need to go on a diet. The elevator can barely hold your weight.*>

<*Why is it my weight? It could be your weight.*>

<*It's your weight because you are the one on a steady diet of meat.*>

<*Meat is life. That word diet sounds painful. Will you go on a diet too?*>

<*Why do I need to go on a diet?*>

<*You are looking thin. Are you eating enough?*>

<*Of course I eat enough. We're not talking about me here.*>

<*If you ate more meat, you would be happier. That's why the angry man is angry. He only eats leaves.*>

He did have a point.

Monty pressed the ground-floor button and looked down the hall at Roxanne as the doors closed.

"You know she cares for you, right?" I said as they closed.

"Yes. I do." He pinched the bridge of his nose. "It's just too complicated and too dangerous."

"I get it." I nodded. "What did Yat say?"

"Not much, he was being deliberately cryptic on the phone."

"This is Yat we're taking about. He's always cryptic. I think they record him for fortune cookie messages."

"You should share that with him, I think he'd enjoy that."

"No, thanks," I said. "Not in the mood to get thwacked today. Pass."

We arrived at the ground floor and the elevator slid open with another soft chime. I saw Yat standing in the lobby of Haven, looking out the window. He turned to us when he heard the chime of the elevator arriving and gave us a short nod.

I looked over at the thin older man and involuntarily winced when I saw him holding a staff. I didn't know how old Yat was, but he never appeared to age.

His slight build hid his immense strength and unbelievable speed. The last time I'd seen Yat, he wore his hair long. Now it was cropped short—a glowing white crown reflecting the sunlight coming in from the windows in the lobby. His eyes were still the same: deep, dark, and unreadable.

We got off the elevator. I was looking across the lobby when I felt the shift in energy. Yat must have sensed it too, because his expression darkened as he leaped over the furniture and headed our way. I pressed the main bead on my mala bracelet, pulling up my shield.

I turned fast and pushed Monty back into the elevator.

"What are you doing?" Monty asked, stumbling back.

I grabbed Peaches by the collar and pulled him behind my shield as I backed up. The energy shift increased and I felt the sensation of ants crawling on my arms.

"Yat has friends," I said, holding up the shield. "The angry kind."

Yat dived over a set of chairs and rolled into a crouch next to me. "Prepare," he said under his breath.

"Simon, don't be ridicu—" Monty started when an immense orb of black energy crashed through the windows and exploded in the lobby.

Thank You!

If you enjoyed this book, would you please help
me by leaving a review at the site where you
purchased it from? It only needs to be a sentence
or two and it would really help me out a lot!

All of My Books

The Warriors of the Way
The Karashihan* • Spiritual Warriors • The Ascendants
• The Fallen Warrior • The Warrior Ascendant • The
Master Warrior

John Kane
The Deepest Cut* • Blur

Sepia Blue
The Last Dance* • Rise of the Night

Chronicles of the Modern Mystics
The Dark Flame • A Dream of Ashes

Montague & Strong Detective Agency
Tombyards & Butterflies• Full Moon Howl•Blood Is
Thicker• Silver Clouds Dirty Sky • Homecoming•
NoGod is Safe•The Date•The War Mage

Night Warden
Wander

*Books denoted with an asterisk are FREE via
my website.*
www.OrlandoASanchez.com

ACKNOWLEDGMENTS

I'm finally beginning to understand that each book, each creative expression usually has a large group of people behind it. This story is no different. So let me take a moment to acknowledge my (very large) group:

To Dolly: my wife and biggest fan. You make all of this possible and keep me grounded, especially when I get into my writing to the exclusion of everything else. Thank you, I love you.

To my Tribe: You are the reason I have stories to tell. You cannot possibly fathom how much and how deep I love you all.

To Lee: Because you were the first audience I ever had. I love you sis.

To the Logsdon family: JL your support always demands I bring my A-game and produce the best story I can. I always hear: "Don't rush!" in your voice.

L.L. (the Uber Jeditor) your notes and comments turned this story from good to great. I accept the challenge!

Your patience knows no bounds. Thank you both.

Arigatogozaimasu

The Montague & Strong Case Files Group AKA- The MoB(The Mages of BadAssery)

When I wrote T&B there were fifty-five members in The MoB. As of this writing there are 608 members in the MoB. I am honored to be able to call you my MoB Family. Thank you for being part of this group and M&S. You each make it possible.

THANK YOU.

WTA-The Incorrigibles

JPL,BenZ, EricQK, S.S.

They sound like a bunch of badass misfits because they are. My exposure to the slightly deranged and extremely deviant brain trust that you are made this book possible. I humbly thank you and…it's all your fault.

The English Advisory

Aaron, Penny, Carrie

For all things English..thank you.

DEATH WISH COFFEE

Kane & Sierra- Thank you!

Is there any other coffee on the face of the earth that can compare? I think not.

<u>To Deranged Doctor Design</u>

Kim. Darja, Milo

You define professionalism and creativity. Thank you for the great service and amazing covers.

YOU GUYS RULE!

<u>To you the reader:</u>

Thank you for jumping down the rabbit hole with me. I truly hope you enjoy this story. You are the reason I wrote it.

ART SHREDDERS

No book is the work of just one person. I am fortunate enough to have an excellent team of readers and shredders who give of their time and keen eyes to provide notes, insight, and corrections. They help make this book go from good to great. Each and every one of you helped make this book fantastic.

THANK YOU

Alex S. Amanda H. Amy R. Andrew W. Audra V. M. Barbara H. Bennah P. Beverly C. Brandy D. Brenda Nix L. Caroline L. Carrie Anne O. Cassandra H. Charlotte C. Chris B. Chris C II. Chris H. Claudia L-S. Corrine L. Daniel P. Darren M. David M. Davina N. Dawn McQ. M. Denise K. Donald T.

Made in the USA
Coppell, TX
26 September 2021

Donna Y. Elizabeth M. Gina G-M. Greg
L. C. Hal B. Helen D. Helen V. Jan G.
Janice K. Jen C. Jim S. Jolene P.
Joscelyn S. Kandice S. Karen H Karen
H. Karla H. Kevin M. Kimbra S. Kisten
B.W. Klaire T. Larry Diaz T. Laura
Cadger R. Laura Maria R. Laurie D.
Lesley S. Leslie D.Y. Linda W. Liz C.
Mark M. Marie McC. Mary Anne P.
MaryAnn S. Marydot Hoffecker P.
Melody DeL. Mike H. Natalie F. Nick
C. Noah S. Oddegeir O L. RC B. Rene
C. Richard L. Robert"The Question" W.
Samantha L. Sara Mason B. Sharon H.
Shawnie N. Stacey S. Stephanie C. Sue
W. Tami C. Tammy Ashwin K. Tammy T.
Tehrene H. Terri A. Thomas R. Timothy
L. Tommy O. Tracy K. Tracy M. Trish V.
B. Violet F. Wendy S.

ABOUT T

Orlando Sanchez has
teens when he was in
for playing Dungeon
every weekend. An a
too numerous to list
prominent are: J.R.R
Richardson, Terry P
Moore,Terry Brooks
George Lucas, And
name a few in no pa

The worlds of his l
twist of the parano
scenes and generou
and mayhem.

Aside from writing
two distinct styles
studying some asp
arts philosophy.

He currently resid
and children and
Starbucks where

Please visit his si
more informatio
releases.

ART SHREDDERS

No book is the work of just one person. I am fortunate enough to have an excellent team of readers and shredders who give of their time and keen eyes to provide notes, insight, and corrections. They help make this book go from good to great. Each and every one of you helped make this book fantastic.

THANK YOU

Alex S. Amanda H. Amy R. Andrew W. Audra V. M. Barbara H. Bennah P. Beverly C. Brandy D. Brenda Nix L. Caroline L. Carrie Anne O. Cassandra H. Charlotte C. Chris B. Chris C II. Chris H. Claudia L-S. Corrine L. Daniel P. Darren M. David M. Davina N. Dawn McQ. M. Denise K. Donald T.

Donna Y. Elizabeth M. Gina G-M. Greg
L. C. Hal B. Helen D. Helen V. Jan G.
Janice K. Jen C. Jim S. Jolene P.
Joscelyn S. Kandice S. Karen H Karen
H. Karla H. Kevin M. Kimbra S. Kisten
B.W. Klaire T. Larry Diaz T. Laura
Cadger R. Laura Maria R. Laurie D.
Lesley S. Leslie D.Y. Linda W. Liz C.
Mark M. Marie McC. Mary Anne P.
MaryAnn S. Marydot Hoffecker P.
Melody DeL. Mike H. Natalie F. Nick
C. Noah S. Oddegeir O L. RC B. Rene
C. Richard L. Robert"The Question" W.
Samantha L. Sara Mason B. Sharon H.
Shawnie N. Stacey S. Stephanie C. Sue
W. Tami C. Tammy Ashwin K. Tammy T.
Tehrene H. Terri A. Thomas R. Timothy
L. Tommy O. Tracy K. Tracy M. Trish V.
B. Violet F. Wendy S.

ABOUT THE AUTHOR

Orlando Sanchez has been writing ever since his teens when he was immersed in creating scenarios for playing Dungeon and Dragons with his friends every weekend. An avid reader, his influences are too numerous to list here. Some of the most prominent are: J.R.R. Tolkien, Jim Butcher, Kat Richardson, Terry Pratchett, Christopher Moore,Terry Brooks, Piers Anthony, Lee Child, George Lucas, Andrew Vachss, and Barry Eisler to name a few in no particular order.

The worlds of his books are urban settings with a twist of the paranormal lurking just behind the scenes and generous doses of magic, martial arts, and mayhem.

Aside from writing, he holds a 2nd and 3rd Dan in two distinct styles of Karate. If not training, he is studying some aspect of the martial arts or martial arts philosophy.

He currently resides in Queens, NY with his wife and children and can often be found in the local Starbucks where most of his writing is done.

Please visit his site at OrlandoASanchez.com for more information about his books and upcoming releases.

Made in the USA
Coppell, TX
26 September 2021

63017606R00184